Believe in yourself even when no one else does!

Always remember you are your own worst critic!

A.W. The Endless Conflict

Part 2 of the Automiton Wars – The Beginning series.

Dedications

My Mother Cheri Bristow McAnnally, for believing in me and raising me to love what I do.

Brittany Ginsburg for editing and pushing me to work on and finish the series.

Crystal Hollenbeck for being a good friend to help me through rough times.

Preface

The war had drawn to a close a long time ago, when the human races had become extinct. The robotic people had rebuilt a civilization that tried to work with the nature around them, rebuilding forests in the radioactive wastes and reviving dead animals. They knew true peace. The planet knew peace at last.

Much of the world had come to destruction in the war, leaving some places unfit for life organic or not. Even the rain could no longer be trusted as it melted and destroyed everything it touched. The robotic cities had to be built with domes to protect them. These domes made of pure energy allowing only the robotic beings in.

Much of the life on the planet had begun to adapt to the harsh reality of radiation. Many of the creatures the humans knew were no more, instead replaced with something a bit more dangerous.

This was the world that had come from the destruction brought on by the robots leader Jax, a robot who lost his life in the war.

Each city, town, and outpost had a statue dedicated to him. Each one a bit different but each of them showing the bot standing proud with his shini in hand. The capitol city was even named after him.

Its name is Jaxfell.

Jaxfell was a hub of research and the rebuild earth movement. The bots worked hard in this city. Through the time of the city the bots, all bots, had begun to reflect the humans that once were. They donned clothing, found love, and even formed a new religion. It was truly magnificent.

The city was quiet one day, everyone busy about their days. A loud explosion racked the city, shaking it to its core. A few scout bots had returned from scouting out into the wastes to find old knowledge and new life. They came back violently, screaming as they destroyed everything. One of these bots placed an explosive at the base of Jax and blew it shouting "Death to lies!"

These bots were quickly dispersed by the guards of the city, stationed to protect from the hostile organic life.

The leader of the robots inspected them himself.

Johnny had found these bots were different from when they had left, their programming changed indefinitely and their xerophia pods glowing a dark red instead of the normal florescent blue. He called to the chief scouting director and demanded a recall for all the scouts in the field.

There was no recall, only a small reply.

"You have lied to us all, your destruction will come! We are reborn!" Sorton, the appeared leader of the scouting party replied before clicking off his com.

The bots looked at one another before looking back at Johnny. Johnny shook angrily as he thought of the best course of action he could make in this situation.

"Fire up the weapon and robotic factories, we go to destroy them!" Jonny shouted.

Chapter 1 – A New Enemy

A few guard bots where sent out to find the remaining scouts, not to engage just locate. There where 5 of these bots, their bodies augmented from the normal skeleton frames; but with heavy armor, built to withstand the blows from the savage mutated animals that wondered the wastes.

They followed the orders sent from Johnny to follow the path the scouts had been sent to.

"If he keeps giving orders like this, I can understand why they would abandon ship!" One of these bots named Will said chuckling quietly to himself. The other bots chuckled with him.

The moved in unison still, step for step. The location from the last com reading was approaching after their more than 3 day hike.

It was an old factory of some kind, perhaps even a research facility. Much of it seemed destroyed to the bots, each one looked about pointing their blasters in every direction where a threat could come from.

Will walked towards the building alone, looking for any form of movement as he passed destroyed old aircraft and vehicles of some kind. Old, almost antique robotic bodies lay about with bullet holes littering their long rusted bodies.

The area seemed empty, though the remnants of the building seemed the best place to hide in the area. Will motioned back at the other bots to move forward into the building remains. All the while he looked down at the long dead bot, the prominent "CR" insignia on one shoulder where the other said "JX-4" where the rest of the insignia was rusted off of the bot.

A flick in his eye showed an all clear reading, drawing his attention away from the bot at his feet. He moved into the old crumbled rooms, finding surprise the auto doors still tried their hardest to open for him with loud screeching of dying gears.

He looked around at the decrepit old human building. He sent off a long range reading back to Jaxfell, showing no enemies found. In return a retreat order came back.

Will motioned for the other bots to move back, a few of them playing with old machinery as the order came through. His eyes fell back to the old bot once more, something about it seemed wrong. Unlike the other bots this one seemed to be moved recently, a closer inspection showed scratches in the concrete next to it, leading back to a small nearly invisibly marked square.

The other bots continued moving as Will looked down at the square, prodding it with his hand, finding he concrete moved slightly. Before he could do anything the door flew open, the muzzle of a shini directly in his face, then nothingness.

* * *

Sorton looked down at the bodies of the fallen bots, many of them still in mid turn as they fell. He motioned for the other bots to move the bodies back into the underground cavern they had found. He stepped in behind them, looking around at the old weapons factory they had found, some antique weapons still sitting in their seeming final places.

Sorton looked around at the few scout bots that stayed with him, checking in with a couple on the status of getting the old machinery fired back up to continue building new bots from the old parts. They gave him thumbs up.

He nodded to himself knowing that he would soon have his army to destroy those who had lied and corrupted the robotic race of beings.

* * *

Sorton watched as old style bodies pumped from the machinery, using whatever materials and parts they could find to fill them. One by one they came out, eyes glowing red as they came to life and walked away, examining their hands as they saw them for the first time. Many of them were made of simple skeleton frames and others were built with heavier armor, as the manufacturing machine built them each for their own purpose. A few of them even came with mixed or missing parts, each of these gathering in their own corner away from the others.

As the weeks passed more than 600 of these beings came to life, pre-programmed with their purpose and orders from Sorton.

He gathered them together in the massive underground hanger, seemingly made for old aircraft.

"My people, we have grown strong over these weeks of building and gathering. Each of you made from the world of the old that we hope to one day bring back. Each of your weapons you hold, made just for you! We will be victorious! We are many while they are few! To war!" Sorton shouted to them all raising his hands in the air to be greeted with a mix of humanist cheering and robotic static.

Chapter 2- Awakening of Soldiers.

Johnny looked through the files the guards had managed to send before their destruction with confusion and anger filling his circuits. He recognized the guerilla tactics that had been used by these bots as the same that the ninja squad had used back in the human war.

He crushed the databoard in his hands, the small fractured pieces scattering about the ground with small tinks as each piece landed.

"Have we any progress with the factories being redesigned for soldiers and weaponry yet?" He shouted at one of the lowly droids that pattered away at a data console.

"Yes sir, we have re-configured one of the agriculture machineries into a vehicle factory, adjusted the waste explorers weapons to be more designated towards armed conflict, and are currently finishing the guard factory into a bot factory. A few of us even have deigned different bot layouts for conflict." The droid chirped out with its primitive voice speaker, still hammering away at the data console. "We should be fully operational by the end of the day."

Johnny patted the droid on its back and over looked the designs for the new bots. Their design ingenious, some made for close range with heavy armor, others made for long range and speed combat with light armor and foot boosters. He liked what he saw; but one thing seemed to bother him.

"Why only 1 eye?" he asked the droid, who did not lose a single press in his sequence.

"The one eye allows better vision being placed in the center, though it can affect depth perception it makes it more so that the bot can see everything as…" The droid clicked the eye on the display next to Johnny. "The entire eye, unlike mine or yours, is the vision camera allowing full scope of vision. We have already created in the bots systems a compensation for depth perception in aim and hand eye coordination."

Johnny nodded as the droid continued to go over the schematics of each of the bots, labeling them shini bot, blaster bot, plasma bot, energy bot, shoti bot, launcher bot, and basher bot. He liked what he heard, understand each of their purposes.

A loud alarm sounded in the command room drawing Johnny's attention. A guard bot popped into the alert screen.

"Johnny sir, we have readings from one of the missing guard bots, its system is down but its recording is still running. The enemy is building new bots on old human equipment sir." The guard paused.

"Any idea of the number Koro?" Johnny asked, his fist clenching behind the droid as it continued working on the new bots programming.

"No sir, the production has been going non-stop it seems for nearly 2 hours." Koro responded.

Johnny fought the urge to punch the droid. "Thank you Koro." He replied as he clicked the screen off.

He sat in silence, the only faint sound the droid finishing their algorithms and coding for the bots.

"I want the changes made in 1 hour" he said as he walked away.

*   *   *

A few of the old bots from the human war gathered around in an old unused building deep in the cities center, what used to be a plant cloning facility. The looked at one another for the first time in many years. A few of them had fallen into a near lifeless state.

"So robots are killing robots now?" Yuro, an old house cleaning bot asked, tapping his one remaining finger on the table between them all as long dead plant life fell from its bottom. "Jax would not stand for this!"

The other bots agreed, some nodding while others with still functioning voice boxes said "Here here".

"Now Johnny is calling for war? Building new shiny bots to kill each other? I will not stand for this! We must go, find these rebel bots and try to stop this before it begins!" Yuro slammed his hand on the table this time, causing a few hiding creatures to jump and scatter.

The door burst open behind him, drawing everyone's attention, blaster fire littering the air with a lazers burning the air around them. Yuro fell to the ground as his head fell from the body. He recorded a metallic foot in front of his face as his mind went dark.

* * *

The factories had become fully operational, pumping one after another of each of the bots for the next few days, building more than 30 of each kind. For each bot 2 weapons had been made. The machinery had even remade the spider tanks from the human war, modifying them slightly in that they were sentient instead of driven.

Johnny had been watching them as they marched out, their programming built for combat made them a fair bit more prepared than the bots in the human wars.

He had summoned the surviving members of the bots from that war, at least the ones he could find, to see the army rise.

"My friends, we have our army." Johnny said as he turned to face the others. "We can not only take out the enemy forces, those rebel bots, we can also take back the wastes and progress the rebuilding of the planet farther!"

One of the more functional bots came forward. Johnny knew him from the war, as he was one of the bots he had run into after leaving the final battle of the war.

"Yes but Johnny, would this be what Jax wanted? Bot killing bot? We fought not to fight but for peace. Why not sit and talk with the rebels instead? Why not be diplomatic?" Carson asked, placing his hand on Johnny's shoulder.

Johnny shrugged the hand off and looked him square in the eyes. "We cannot simply talk with them! They came to our cities and destroyed our home! The raised arms against our peace! They must be destroyed!"

Carson shook his head and rejoined the other bots. "For this, you will sacrifice us all!" Carson turned back to look at Johnny "Unlike the humans, these are our kind! They will rebuild as we will, and this war will continue through to the end of time." Carson turned back and continue walking, the other bots joining him.

Johnny shook his head as he turned back to his now ever growing army. "They know not what they say. Our army will destroy them and then reclaim the wastes!" One of the droids who designed the new bots came up to him by surprise, the droid engine running nearly silent.

"Johnny" is said, causing him to jump slightly. "We have new readings on the rebels! We count only 600 of them. The dorn a new marking though, as if to mark them as different. It seems to be a nut surrounded by a read glowing light. Should we do the same?"

Johnny thought back to the humans stories he had read before the war had ended. He remembered war banners and national flags being the things that humans would use to show where they had come from or fought for.

"Yes, but make ours different. They put a nut, we put a wrench, and make it golden! We are the just, we are the originals! We built them, so we can destroy them!" Johnny sent the droid off. He looked over his army and scoffed to himself. "Red versus blue, seems to be almost a cliché."

*   *   *

Carson and the others moved in unison to their old hangout, hoping to find the missing bots. They had not seen Yuro and his party since before their call to meet up with Johnny. The moved towards the old familiar building that housed an old plant cloning set-up. They found the door broken down, something that instantly alerted them to foul play.

Carson pulled out his concealed old blaster pistol, something he had not used since the human wars. He stepped in to find the carnage of a battle, blaster and lazer burns littering the building, bits of metal scraps from the beings they knew as friends.

Carson looked closely around, looking for any complete bot, only to find none. Whom ever had brought the fight into the building had left only scraps.

The bot looked back at his comrades shaking his head.

"We know why they did not come now. Who could have done this?" Carson asked, the other bots just staring dumb founded at him.

They stepped away from the old building. Bits of flashing from the dome alerted them that it was raining out in the wastes.

"Would Johnny be so desperate for war he would kill those who opposed is?" Carson asked himself in his mind.

*   *   *

Sorton watched as the rain fell thinking about the days to come. The rain had always fascinated him, remembering stories about before the human war where the rain was not deadly and humans would play in it. He longed for those days, though he had never been there.

He thought back to when he was a lowly scout, searching the wastes for remnants of life to save or knowledge lost to time. It was no life he had wanted, but it was the purpose for which he was built. Like so many others he had known from Jaxfell and the other cities, the bots wished for so much more than what had been provided to them.

Each of them had been imprinted with the stories from the war, about Jax the savior of the Automiton race. He hoped to change this, hoped to bring an end to the control from Johnny, the lies from the past.

Chapter 3 – A War of Untold Horror

Gizmin walked with his fellow bots off to war, a fresh imprint of a golden wrench adorning their shoulders like the humans of the past. They did not know what awaited them in the wastes or in the battles to come, only what Johnny had told them to do. They had been simple orders, destroy the rebels and return home.

Something told Gizmin this was not going to be so easy. He was a low end blaster bot, a model he knew was meant to be expendable. The first ones to go into battle, followed by the others. He did not like this, but would do nothing about it, for he knew that he would be different than the others. He would survive the battles.

The city's end was coming, the power dome pulsating around them. They walked through, the feeling of extra electricity powered them farther, almost to an overloading level. It lasted for only a few steps before the wastes sat before them.

Through all of the effort of the bots, the surrounding areas of the city seemed to be nothing but desert. The ground cracked from the immense heat, the little living plant life withered and crumbled. It was something new for all of them to see, though they could not linger on it for too long as they had a job to do. They needed to finish the mission, end the war before it could grow farther than it already had.

The bots walked for nearly 3 days, passing through different waste areas, almost stumbling into an electro zone, a few shut down forever stuck in walking position. Gizmin looked at the poor bots stuck there, no others seeming to notice. He looked at the other bots who walked with him.

"How can they not feel sad for this happening?" he asked himself as he shook his head and moved on, the newly arriving grass beneath him crunching to bits with each step.

Another day's journey had them almost to where they needed to go; but something had come into their path they did not know how to handle. A large flowing river cut their path, satellite readings showed it would be a more then 4 days journey to its end. Gizmin looked around quietly as the others tried to determine the best course of action. A few of the shini bots, the leader class, debated on it. Gizmin noticed something from the corner of his eye. A few small crewed rafts sat next to the water, hidden by the remnants of an old human vehicle.

"Why not take those?" Gizmin asked the others, extending out his figure to point at the rafts. The shini bots looked over the rafts, inspecting to see if they would be sufficient enough to carry the army over.

"You blaster G-35" The shini bot pointed at Gizmin. "You take a raft to the other side, ensure they are safe."

Gizmin ignored the shini bot's rudeness and nodded, jumping into the raft. He grabbed the sides quickly as it bobbed up and down in the water, a new sensation to the bot. He flicked at the small mechanical device he assumed was a motor in the back of the raft. A quick xerophia glow from it kicked in as a part of the metal shifted away, and the raft was off. The thing fired through the river, almost gliding over its surface. Gizmin held on for life, as he knew if he fell over the water would destroy him almost instantly.

He had reached the other side rather quickly, the raft crashing into the shore without a care. He sent a short range signal to the others, letting them know it was safe. Within seconds, the 3 other rafts fired across the water, bringing more blaster bots and a few shoti bots. Then the rafts were sent back across. This happened a few times before the shini and sniper bots turn.

As the shini and sniper bots crossed, something popped from out of the water. A large tentacle grabbed blindly at the bots, grabbing a few of the shini bots and pulled them under the water. They didn't even have a chance to scream.

The wastes were frightening to Gizmin, everything adapting to kill the other things. He wanted to get the mission over with and return home to never come out again.

* * *

Sorton watched the old monitors for the defense systems, only a few of them still semi functioning. They showed a large number of beings moving towards the base, few disappearing into the river. The other scouts that had come with him sat watching as well, each of them no doubtedly having devious thoughts of what to do about these intruders.

"Keep the troops back until they are right outside our doors, then spring the trap and end them." Sorton said turning of the screen before flipping around to look sat the other scout bots. "They will never see this coming."

*   *   *

Gizmin followed behind the group, looking around at what he could only describe in his mind as an old town, though only parts of walls remained standing. There was not too say about the location; yet he found himself compelled to feel bad for any living thing that had been here when the destruction had come. An old bent metal structure sat in a pool of what must have at one time been sand. What appeared to be a ladder, broken and rusted as it was, lead to a small platform before a metal shoot lead out to the ground. The idea of it confused him, without knowing its original use, though he knew it must have something to do with a child human as a few remnants of dolls lay scattered around the structure.

He looked back at the other bots to find not a single one of them had paused to look back at the echoes from the past. He had, during this journey, began to question the other bots and himself. It seemed to him that the others did not have understanding or curiosity beyond that of the mission.

He continued walking with them none the less, as they had a mission to complete.

It took the group just a few hours before they arrived at the area where the other bots had gone missing. Gizmin looked around from a distance, his eye display telling him he needed to get to the front for potential battle. He did not want to though, as his mind had already been made up that something was not right about this place.

Before he or the others could notice several snaps filled the air before large electrified nets slammed against portions of the army, their bodies convulsing on the ground. A few shots where let off by the convulsing bots, sending a few more bots to the ground. The bots who had been shot lay on the ground quickly, eyes flickering off.

Gizmin hid behind the only thing he could find around him, an old aircraft. As his shoulder touched the machine, a skeletal hand fell to the ground from the rusted hole in its side.

Gunfire exploded behind the craft, as odd looking bots flew from what seemed to be the ground itself. Many of the bots Gizmin had come with fell to the ground quickly as bits of their bodies fell away. In the distance a crack sounded off, followed in short successions with others. Many of the bots who flooded from the ground exploded in a mix of sparks and metal debris.

A loud whistling surrounded Gizmin as a few rockets flew past, the explosion sending the craft into his side. He stumbled to the ground, dropping his blast to catch himself. He arose to a large amount of shock as robotic body parts and coolant filled everything around him, a few of the limbs still twitching.

He looked back at where the shots had come from to look for his allies to rally with him. They had been nowhere to be seen, as was their programming sets. He sent a short range broadcast on their private channels.

"We need to regroup and progress together." He said to the unseen bots.

"You are alone out there blaster? We have readings of others moving close by." A sniper replied.

Gizmin looked about himself, seeing no moving or functioning bot remaining in the gore.

"There is no other bots here." Gizmin sent back to the sniper.

"We will be there in." the line cut off. Loud cracks exploded in the air before everything went silent.

He tried a few more short range broadcasts to no response. There was no other bot he could call ally remaining and he knew it. He quickly grabbed for his blaster, not knowing when the enemies would come to clear the mess.

It turned out not long as no sooner had his finger slipped by the trigger as the ground began to open up, more bots flooding out. They saw him, gun fire filling the air. He could feel a few click past his armored shell as he returned fire. He managed to take down 3 of them, their heads exploding from the blaster overload shots he sent through the air.

A plasma shot caught his leg though, sending his metallic body scrapping against the concrete, sparks scattering in fear. He could not raise his arm back in time to return fire before another plasma shot hit his arm, melting the joint clean through, the arm clacking to the ground. He looked back up from his downed arm at the bot standing before him, a laz pistol staring him directly in the eye.

"Death to lies." The bot said.

A bright light followed by intense heat then nothing.

Chapter 4 – A Low Expectation

Sorton looked at the remnants of the new bots, inspecting their destroyed bodies.

"A single eye with heavy armor for most, light armor for others?" He shook his head. "It seems we had the same thought in building ours."

Sorton looked over to a few of the bots he had created, motioning for them to come over. They did not hesitate as their feet flew them over. A small salute as they stopped.

"Take these bots, melt them down, and put the remains into our forges. I feel we will be needing it soon. Same goes for our fallen." He patted one on the shoulder. "We will need quite a few of you guys."

The bots took a few minutes to move the dead out from the room towards the forges. Sorton watched as the last leg dragged across the ground out the door.

Again he was alone in the command room, a few of the instruments making beeping and flashing. Sorton had done something that even the humans could not do during the wars. He had defeated an army of robots with very little casualties on his side.

He looked over at the instruments only partly paying attention to them as he continued to think to himself.

"Johnny will come back, his army larger and stronger. We will need to prepare." He said to himself. He pushed a few buttons on the command console, a flashing light on the screen reading "building commencing" began to flicker. "We will need to attack."

*   *   *

Johnny hit the back of the droid in anger, the small thing not even noticing. The readings for the last of the bots flicked off on the screen.

"I thought you had designed these bots for combat against other bots!" He shouted at the droid, striking it once more. "Build them better! Build them more durable!"

The droid just continued to type at the console, not saying a word back to Johnny. This just fueled his anger farther. He could not afford to destroy the droid, this he knew, so instead he walked back towards his desk. He slammed his hand clean through the steel desk top, feeling a few of the joints in his hand crack apart.

"Ramp up production of the spider tanks and warwings." He shouted to another droid.

The droid nodded and typed a few commands into their console.

Johnny could not believe what had happened, losing his whole advanced army to an army made of nothing but old recycled parts. He stared at the flashing blue prints for the bots. They were perfect, made of the best materials they could make in mass production, yet taken out so easily.

"Transmit the views of the bots to my databoard!" He shouted at the first droid. He needed to know what had caused the destruction so quickly.

*   *   *

Johnny trembled with the databoard in his hand, watching the views once more.

"Electric net traps?!" He shouted at the droid. "They fell for an electric net trap? Did you not build them to think?!"

The droid for the first time stopped its typing, turning back to Johnny.

"The thought of the soldiers is just to follow orders, and destroy. Not of self-preservation, and not of learning like you or I!" The droid shouted at Johnny, causing him to lean back in his chair. "This is the most efficient way to complete the mission!"

Johnny stared at the droid in silence for a few moments before laughing quietly. The droid seemed confused, looking around for the source of the joke.

"You say no self-preservation or learning like us ey?" He chuckled. The droid stayed silent, just staring directly into Johnny's eyes. "Then explain this!" Johnny slid the databoard over to the droid.

The droid watched it with confusion, tilting its head.

"This bot, Gizmin he called himself, was much like us. Hiding from the destruction, stopping to inspect things to learn about them! This is not what you described!" Johnny shouted at the droid, slamming his hand on the desk once more.

The droid looked over the footage several times before placing the databoard down, bowing his head at Johnny.

"I cannot explain what caused this Gizmin to be made sir; but I can assure you that this will not happen again!" The droid began to go back to the console it had endlessly typed at.

"No you fool, make the others more like him!" Johnny shouted, something he was finding himself doing more and more of since the initial attack.

"Sir?"

"He survived the longest of the bots, evaded attacks multiple times, and found solutions to problems the others simply gave up on!" Johnny chuckled.

The droid nodded slightly, still seeming confused with what Johnny was hinting at. "So sir, you want the bots all to be like this Gizmin? Fully functional like us?"

Johnny nodded slightly "yes, what good is a soldier if they do not care for what they fight?"

*   *   *

The droid Servo did as Johnny had asked of him, taking the base programming for the new bots and implementing full functionality. One thing did bother him through his work though. "How did Gizmin come to be?" He asked himself as he completed the final programming changes.

"Inefficient choice, these bots will run I fear instead of completing the missions laid before them." Servo thought, closing the command file. "Once that happens, he will have me revert it back."

Servo nodded to Johnny to signal it had been finished.

"It's only a matter of time before the bots get changed back to my perfect soldiers." He thought once more as he sent the new bot programming to all of the factories to be put in the bots.

*   *   *

Sorton looked through the old file matrix of the hidden factory, more out of boredom than anything. It had been nearly 2 days since the army had been sent off to fight the cities and outposts in close adjacent to them. The signal scans showed

Johnny had not alerted the other cities or outposts of the conflict.

The bots under his control did not fully understand his request to attack and destroy the towns. He himself did not fully understand it either, as he was simply following the strategies found in the very matrix he was looking through.

After a long while of scrolling through the systems a file stood out, catching his eye. A file named Fenrir. He remembered reading about the mythical beast in the history files found in the matrix; but could not understand why there would be a file under the military systems dedicated to the beast.

Curiosity got the best of him, clicking through the file after a few moments of thought. The blue prints of the satellite weapon astonished him. He knew this weapon would be perfect to attack the other robots, cutting his own casualties short.

The file stated to him the weapon had been built and used before already, seemingly against bots in the human wars.

"With this Johnny would not stand a chance" he thought to himself. He quickly began research through the file on how the weapon was used, hoping to find something that could make it functional.

*　　　　　　*　　　　　　*

Reports had come in from several other cities and outposts of attacks similar to that at Jaxfell. Each telling of the bots attacking and destroying everything they could, eyes glowing an evil red. A few of the smaller outposts had fallen and been taken over by the enemies who had announced their new name as "The Rebirthed".

The bots in charge of each city and outpost pleaded to Johnny for direction, as many of them did not even have the basic ability to defend themselves.

Johnny listened to their pleas for help, one by one. It was almost unbearable to hear. He replied to them all to have a meeting over the video coms, hoping to settle things down and perhaps build a new strategy as the ones he had tried over the last few weeks had not worked, losing countless bots to battles.

As the meeting started, Johnny stood in the center of the com room, the leaders each dedicated to their own single screen, surrounded him. The chattering and yelling began fairly quickly, most of them screaming and yelling about needing weaponry. Johnny quickly raised his hands to silence them all. The room fell silent almost instantly.

"I understand we have all been under siege from these Rebirthed. We here at Jaxfell have been working hard on a solution to the problem, building up weaponry to crush them where they stand." Johnny lowered his hands. "We have had several….misshapes in attempting to end this." The crowd began to roar once more.

"What do you mean misshapes?" One yelled.

"You have weaponry but haven't shared it?" Another shouted.

"You knew about the Rebirthed before they attacked us all?" Shouted another.

The crowd began to become angrier by the second.

Johnny slammed his hand against the wall, drawing all of their attention.

"Yes we knew of the Rebirthed before the attacks. We have been slowly waring with them for a few months now, to little success. I called you all to this meeting to set up a strategy, and to present you with our findings." Johnny paused, looking at the others as they looked at one another. "We have found where they are coming from, though we have not been able take them down. They have taken refuge in an old human weapons factory and research facility. Their leader, designating himself Sorton, is smart about his fighting." An image of Sorton shared to the screens. "He has taken out every bot we have sent at him, without losing more than a handful of their own bots. He has adapted to the old strategies."

One of the bots in the meeting blurted out. "Why not just strike the facility with heavy weaponry from the skies? We have been told by your little droid aircraft have been created for things of that nature."

Johnny looked over at Servo, who quickly scurried out of the room.

"The only concern with that is this." The screen with Sorton's face changed to a rough image of the facility where the Rebirthed hid. "This facility was built to withstand attacks from above. It survived blasts from bombs during the wars, as well as housed them. It would be futile to bomb at it. Instead we have to take it.." the screen changed to the river "with nature as our ally. If we can flood it, they would either be trapped inside of destroyed by the water."

The bots in the meeting nodded in understanding, a few of them whispering to bots hidden from the screens.

"This doesn't answer the concern of us not having weaponry though." One of them chimed in.

Johnny nodded, clicking at the console on the wall. Each of the bots screens now displayed the blueprints of bots, weapons, and vehicles.

"These are the blueprints we have created for our army, we have already broadcast them to the factories in the bigger cities. We will be constructing them and shipping them out to the smaller outposts for defense." The bots all cheered with excitement. "This meeting is adjourned."

Johnny clicked the screens off before falling to the floor.

"With any luck, we can stop the Rebirthed before they find that weapon." He looked over at the console still showing the image of the all too familiar facility.

Chapter 5- Reinforcements Have Arrived

Over the next few weeks the bots had been built and delivered in small quantities to the different cities and outposts. The attacks had come more frequently at these outposts, a few of them falling to the Rebirthed.

The leaders all pleaded for more and more bots to be sent, for fear of the factories falling to the enemy. Each cry met with new troops.

A few spider tanks had even been dispatched to the cities for a stationary weapon defense. All the while, the scouting missions still continued into the wastes, as even with the war going on the mission of gathering the history and saving the planets organic life continued.

One of these scouts is named Brit.

*   *   *

Brit looked over the remains of an old mall, bits of it still looking relatively intact as moss grew over its walls. She scooped up a bit of the moss, unable to determine the type from just look. She slid some of it into a small storage vile in the bag she kept on her left side, made from bits of old nylon. The rest she examined closely, scanning it against the data she had on moss. No matches had been found, determining this was a new breed of it.

She continued into the mall, cleaning her hands on the way in to prevent cross contamination of the plant life. The insides of the mall were far more intact. Most of the stores still had remnants of their original purposes, donning products the humans did not deem needed still littering the shelves.

The old tile flooring had cracked though, some dead plant life making its way through the cracks log ago to die in the unlivable mall.

"Shame" Brit said, examining the remnants of some form of shrubbery.

She continued through her exploration of the mall, A few old objects catching her attention here and there. One of these objects continually kept distracting her. It was a small metal and, what seemed to use to be, plastic contraption. She could not fight her curiosity any further, grabbing at the object, snatching it from the shelf of some form of electronics store.

She cleaning it off, an odd long faded green logo embroidered on its side with the name Morphodox just beneath it.

She examined it closely, finding a few small buttons that seemed to still be working on its side, as well as an old primitive power plug leading from it.

She pulled an old adapter from her bag, the xerophia end of it dark from not being used. With a quick flick of her wrist she snapped the adapter to the old device, the xerophia dome lighting a dim blue.

A small light flicked on the device, a hologram with the same symbol from its side began to spin over its top.

Brit stared at this item with delight, something she had not experienced much since the fighting had begun. The logo changed to a selection screen of some kind, a few titles for programs floating where the logo once was.

"House of Nightmares, Legendary Maze, Storm the Fort, Survive the Trifits?" She read with confusion. She turned the small device off, not wanting to waste more time.. She slipped it into the bag with the others. "I will need to check what those programs are for later."

She continued on through the mall, noting a few smaller insects and animals scurrying about in the dead plant life.

"Some promise" she thought as she noticed a set of eyes peering from one of the darkened stores, a small growl emitting from it.

Without hesitation she moved towards it, hand on her blaster in case it was another of the mutated monstrosities. The light from her xerophia dome lit the area as she walked up to it, revealing the creature bit by bit.

Its paws where adorned with large claws, a few seemingly chipped from unknown fights with unknown enemies. Its fir a dim green, bits of it missing from either fights or radiation exposure. Its body was rather small, malnourished looking; no doubt from the lack of other creatures in the wastes. Last its face, what seems to at one point been a wolf of some kind, was sunken in, long broken teeth gnarled in either fear or anger. Its 4 eyes stared out at Brit, watching her every move.

    She knew the creature had been mutated, but she was not sure to what extent it had. The creature seemed to be more upset with her being there than vicious. She took her free hand to the pouch on her right side, snatching out a few pieces of cloned meat for the creature, tossing them a bit from it to force it out of its hiding place.

The creature did not hesitate in the slightest, leaping from the darkness, giving Brit a nice look at its 6 seemingly backwards legs. The creature devoured the meat as if it had not eaten in weeks. Its 2 tails wagged back and forth. With a better look at the creature, Brit noticed the large spines sticking from its back, each seemingly serrated to prevent being eaten by another predator.

The creature was beautiful to her, a sight of true survival evolution, artificial as it was from the radiation. She offered it more meat, this time keeping it in her hands to draw it closer.

The creature did not hesitate to come closer, eating the meat straight from her hands. It showed no fear. Her hand pet the creature gently, the thing seemingly enjoying it. After a short bit of examining and petting the creature, Brit walked away, seeking to find more life out of the mall.

The creature followed her.

*　　　　　*　　　　　*

Sorton looked over their newly setup monitoring systems, a few of them tapping into long dormant spy satellites from the paranoid humans while others viewed cameras they had placed on out exploring missions.

He looked these over, watching as the enemy bots had reinforced their cities and outposts, mostly with smaller bots but also something larger. These things, large mechanical spiders, he could only classify as a form of vehicle.

He had explored the weapon files after finishing with the Fenrir weapon, finding blue prints for a few different tanks and other vehicular assault weaponry. Out of them had had found a few that would be sufficient to the cause.

One of these weaponry, similar to the spider weapon, walked instead of rolled, though it only had 4 legs. Mounted to the vehicle though was 2 large mortar-style cannons. Each cannon held a large explosive spreader shell, testing showing it would explode in the air above the target and litter it with over 20 smaller explosions destroying everything in the proximity.

The second a small human sized tank, running on a mix of treads and wheels. It looked similar to a snake in its design, though a bit more crunched. This vehicle was an unmanned device, capable of carrying 2 troops into battle or, with its explosive inside, kamikaze into enemies. Tests of this explosive resembled a small nuclear explosion.

The last, an air based vehicle. It resembled a few of the vehicles on the strip outside of the base with its base design, long narrow body with rudders and thrusters on its tail and wings. The main difference being 2 large swiveling engines, keeping it afloat at a hover. This vehicle, plainly made for transport, had a few large chain guns and a couple of emp cannons equipped to it.

Sorton had begun construction of these as soon as he could after building a few test versions.

"Funny, it seems these where designed to destroy robots and at long last it is what they will be doing." He thought to himself, chuckling slightly at the thought.

Attention was drawn to the screen next to him as radio signals came in from the bots he had sent to take out a small outpost in hopes of finding more building materials.

*   *   *

The bots around Brunner hid in the remains of a few old human vehicles, watching over the night drowned plains at the small outpost in the distance. The strong light from its dome littering the areas around it. Stationed just by its main entrance sat a large vehicle of some sort, seeming to be a large mechanical spider.

Brunner nodded over to the bot aiming down the sights of his lazer sniper. The bot nodded back and fired a single shot.

The spider tank in the distance caught partially on fire, flailing madly looking for the source of the lazer. It fired off a few shots, electricity filling the air just as the shots made impact with a few unoccupied vehicles.

A second shot from the lazer sniper caused the tank to slam against the frame of the domes entrance, sparks flying from the metal on metal contact.

At this point more than 20 bots poured out of the entrance, weapons poised at eye level, tracing their every head movement. A few nearly silent shots erupted from the vehicles, send about 5 of the bots down in the night. The tank made a few more shots out at the vehicles, one of them making its mark as the car with a few bots only equipped with a few blasters flew back, electrical flames replacing the vehicle.

Brunner aimed down his own sites, bringing the plasma cannon to a ready state, a slight beep from the overcharge filling his ears as he squeezed the release. A beam of light slammed into the tank, 3 of its 8 legs melting straight through within seconds, causing the tank to fall to the ground as it fired a shot, blowing itself into nothingness.

The enemy bots now knew where the shots where coming from, returning fire with a mix of shini fire and a few blasters. The vehicle Brunner his within shook with every shot, each bullet punching a new hole through the long rusted frame. The bots around him returned more fire back at them, 6 more falling to the gun fire, the shini fire disappearing from the night.

The plasma weapon signaled ready to fire once more, brining Brunner back to the battle, aiming at the stupidly clustering bots, releasing a few small charges at them. One of the bots screamed out in fear as his legs melted out from beneath him, while the others seemingly just fell as the white hot gunk engulfed their bodies and heads, bubbling the metal like water.

Brunner placed the weapon back to his side, readying his blaster, looking at the remaining bots from his squad who stared back at him. He nodded, and without a word the bots all moved in unison towards the outpost.

*   *   *

Jeron heard the gunfire outside, watching as the energy dome shimmered with bullet ricochets. He could not focus on them long as he needed to finish his work, typing away at his data console. He had been working on something new for Johnny and his droids, a new form of defense. As he finished the last code, the dome collapsed, the energy dissipating into the air. The smaller buildings just outside began to erupt into gunfire and air sizzling. He sent the coding and blueprint off to the capitol with a quick few clicks.

The door burst open behind him, burning metal splattering onto the ground. He had no weapon to defend himself, as he had fool heartedly placed his trust in the guards that had been posted. A few strange looking bots, eyes and xerophia spheres glowing red rushed into the room. He had no time to speak or bargain, the bots filled the air with gunfire, several of the electro shells plowing directly through his un-armored chest. He fell back onto the data console, coolant already beginning to pool beneath him. He slid down to the ground, his arm attempting to brace his fall.

His mind went blank before being able to even hit the ground.

*   *   *

Johnny examined the new blueprints that he had received. The design needed work to him, as it was relatively rudimentary in shape, but the purpose would more than make up for that. He had already decided on first glance that this would make a good addition to the cities for defense, hopefully allowing for more robotic lives to be spared.

The droids next to him did not have to wait for his answer, already going about adjusting the shape of the blueprint to be more efficient.

"Hail Jeron, we need to thank him for his works." Johnny said, sitting down in the chair by the holoscreen.

The droid nodded, sending off the commands for the holo-call.

What appeared on the holoscreen was not Jeron. Johnny sat up rather quickly as the red eyes appeared on the screen.

"So he is dead then?" Johnny asked the Rebirthed bot, trying to disguise the disgust in his voice.

"We have destroyed him, and every bot here. You will not win this war. Death to lies!" The bot disappeared from the screen.

Johnny sat there for a while, saying nothing. The droids around him did not seem to notice, or care as they continued working at their posts.

"Another outpost taken down by these monsters." He thought to himself, restraining himself from hitting the holoscreen next to him. "We will have to push this war forward than."

Johnny quickly jolted to his feet, arm already extended and pointing to the droid next to him.

"You!" he exclaimed, the droid quickly turning to face him. "Double production of the bots, weaponry, tanks, and this new device! We go on the attack once more!"

Johnny barely heard the droids acknowledgement of the order as he stormed off to his quarters. After he arrived there, he quickly sat in his coolant station, an old ammo box in his hands. He quivered slightly at the box, flipping its lid open to reveal a small odd device.

Its tip looked much like the tesla coils of old human times, but its body was a small box with spirals of metal jutting from its bottom.

Electrocharging was not banned or frowned upon in the robotic society, though it was not something normally done. Johnny sighed to himself.

"We will destroy them, and this device will never need to be used again." He said quietly to himself as he jammed the spiraling coils into the coolant station, electricity pouring out from the tesla coil end, arching into his body. His display went haywire and everything began to shut off. It felt so good.

Chapter 6 – A New Arrival

Brit had named the creature, at least to the best of her ability. She named the creature Trunder. The creature had followed her through her whole scouting mission, staying relatively close, but not close enough to touch. It had fended off a few radiated animals of unknown origin when she had ventured into the remains of an old zoo.

Trunder had ripped into ones neck, sending a mix of greenish blood and flesh flying everywhere, some splattering Brit.

She had grown a fondness for the creature, occasionally handing it some small amounts of food over their multiday journey. On the journey she had discovered multiple living old plants and animals; but sadly most she discovered where mutated or destroyed otherwise.

She was on her way back to Jaxfell, as her specimen bag on her left was full, and the bag she had been feeding Trunder from hung empty on her right. She was but a half-day walk from the city when she began to notice her coolant system needed cleaning, as her body was beginning to overheat from the xerophia.

This was of no concern, as she knew she would get there in no time, well before the overheating would take her down. The only thing that began to worry her was the forming clouds in the sky, electricity beginning to fill the air. Even Trunder knew this, as she found it constantly looking for any form of shelter it could take.

She stopped at the first thunder clap, both her and Trunder jumped slightly. She looked at him and him at her.

"Run!" she shouted, hoping the creature had been able to understand her. The surrounding area was empty, no caves or old buildings to be spoken of.

She took off, going at full speed, her coolant system going from an orange warning to red. She could not keep this up for long, yet if she did not the rain would destroy her. Trunder kept right up with her, almost passing her a few times; but stopping slightly to keep pace with her.

A pop on her left sent her flying, as a lightning bolt struck the ground, arching over to her own body. This sent some of her systems into shutdown, making her legs inoperable. The ground gave under her body, breaking up the dried dirt into a small cloud.

An overwhelming sadness began to fill her as she knew she would not make it back or into shelter in time. She felt something touching her arm, drawing her attention from her self-pity.

Trunder rubbed against her, trying to push her back to her feet.

"I'm sorry Trunder, you will have to leave me here." She said, sadness drenching her tone. She pointed down at her legs. "They do not work anymore."

Trunder rubbed against her more, pushing harder and harder. He bit at her arm between each shove. Brit began to believe she knew what he was doing. She wrapped her arm around the creature, pulling herself to its back. As she slid onto its back, Trunder went from a standing position to a full gallop in the same direction they had been going.

Trunder was much faster then she though, going speeds over 65 mph; turning the landscape around them into a blur. The clouds overhead had completely blocked out the sky, a few of them forming into odd looking funnels. The wind was picking up with the funnels growing more and more in size.

Brit watched this, knowing this was no simple rain storm. It was an emp storm, known for taking down anything in its way with large funnel clouds charged with electricity and acid rain.

The claps from the thunder began to grow more frequent, bits of acid rain beginning to pour down to the ground, sizzling the very earth around them.

A single bit touched Trunder's ear, sending the creature into a frenzy, his speed increasing to over 80mph. Its ear began to burn away, blood and burnt flesh falling away and splashing Brit with the stench.

The dome was now visible in the distance, the newly stationed spider tanks at the front entrance.

"Scout NJM-909 coming in with organic specimens at rapid speed. Do not fire, I repeat do not fire. Scout is riding an animal." She broadcast out to the city and spider tanks.

Trunder began to pant heavily, straining to keep the pace up. Brit pet him gently, giving him a bit of encouragement to keep going. "We are almost there." She whispered to him.

"Scout NJM-909 we read you clear. The storm is coming hard, please be cautious on entry. Is the animal hostel?" A reply came back to her, broken up from the electrical storm.

"Negative, creature is not hostile. Be advised, creature is firghtenable." She replied back.

The spider tanks where almost within reach now. Trunder, had begun to slow down, his body shaking under the stress. Brit pet him the best she could, trying to push it just a bit hard.

A blast exploded behind them, sending them both flying to the base of the entrance. Her vision started to fade as her systems overheated, the last thing she saw was a few service droid flying out into the now beginning to pour rain.

*   *   *

Brunner sat looking over the carnage outside from the rain, watching as one of their damaged fell from the acid, bits of the metal beginning to melt away with every passing second. Sparks flew from the electronics as the metal shell gave way. A small muted explosion from the xerophia pod overloading caused a flash into the old cave where they hid.

"Rest now." He whispered to himself as he turned back to the cave. He and his fellow bots had weapons at the ready long before they began to move farther into the cave. Something about this seemed un-natural. Their red xerophia pods and eyes where the only lights in the cave, the rest just out of their radius was pitch black. Examining the ground showed scuffs and scratches, alerting them that they may have a few radiated animals somewhere in the cave to have to deal with. None the less they proceeded forward.

The cave after nearly 100 feet changed from rock to metal, crafted and welded metal. Brunner scouted forwards, requesting the others to hold back.

He snuck forward, pacing his hand against the wall to help brace his movement. After another 50 feet he found what lay on the other side of the cave, an old shanty town of sorts, perhaps left untouched from the human times.

He climbed down the side of the cave to the town, a convenient rusted ladder allowing this to be with ease.

After a short scouting mission he knew this was from the human times, bits of small remnants of clothing and housewares filling the rudimentary buildings. This did not disturb him, what disturbed him was there was no dust, no weathering, nothing on the items in the buildings.

No sounds around him, nothing but his own footsteps. Something still seemed odd though, as a faint light had started to grow in one of the buildings. He moved towards it for investigation, weapon at the ready. What he found he could not believe.

"Get out of the cave if you can. Get as close to the end as you can without being in the rain if not." He sent to his troops.

They did not respond, but that was of no matter. What lay before him was an old energy cell, hooked directly to an old miniature warhead. The timer on the energy cell counted to 0. The explosion was only there for a split second as Brunner's systems shut down, his body melting almost instantly at the intense heat.

*   *   *

Sorton watched at his life readers kicked off for about 12 bots. His hands flew faster than he could realize as he researched into the bots broadcasts to find what had happened.

A few short seconds showed the energy cell and explosion. The others showed running followed by fire and light.

Sorton looked away from the screen, disgusted with what he saw.

"Attention all free bots, we must find what had killed our brethren and destroy it. They threaten our truth!" He broadcast out to all the Rebirthed in the base.

He turned back to the screens, flicking between the bots he had sent to the different surrounding outposts, watching as they one by one either died or destroyed the bots preventing the capture.

"Johnny would not have done that, than who would have?" He asked himself, smashing the consoles side with his fist.

*   *   *

Jared watched the horizon with little interest, wishing he could have something else to do. He had been stationed where he was at the Orotho outpost as punishment for removing the arm of one of the commanding bots. Though the droids found that his emotions programing was a little wonky as the cause, he had committed the crime none the less.

Nothing ever happened at Orotho, as it was a simple scouting outpost. No resources or factories around, and barely any shelter from the storms.

Servo, the droid responsible for the destruction of many bots for being "imperfect" had also been sent to this outpost, one of only a handful of non-guard bots assigned to this outpost. Jared did not really like the droid, as at the trial Servo suggested he be melted down and turned into another bot.

Jared was required to listen to him now though. The droid had gone on and on for days on ways to improve the outpost, and make the armies better. He had even gone a little mad in wanting to capture live rad animals to mechanize them. He was a crazy one.

"And they call me crazy?" he asked himself as the droid hammered away at a guard who was ignoring the orders to run out into he field to gather a bit of the rad animals.

Nothing ever happened at Orotho.

Chapter 7 – Something Wicked in Orotho

"He will regret his decision very quickly indeed." Servo chimed to himself, welding a bit of metal as he angrily mocked Johnny. "Oooh look at me, I'm one of the originals, helped Jax end the war blah blah blah." The little droid mocked.

The weld was made fairly hastily, leaving bits botched here and there. He had been working on this project since the second day stationed out in Orotho;

spending each hour he could fixing it up or gathering parts for it.

Bits of the rad animals had been used in his new creation, mainly limbs and skin. Each part of it held together with bits of metal and wiring, connecting the preserved organs and tissue together.

"My rad-animal cyborg will solve the problems of the wastes and these Rebirthed scum. Blending in with the natural beings to destroy them from within." He ripped a piece of the flesh away, slamming in bits of electrical devices and attaching them to the muscle. "Then he will no longer question my works."

Servo continued with his work on this rad mountain lion, or at least what remained of one. He tossed the excess skins he replaced with metal into the piles of other failed rad-animal cyborgs.

"We just need to get the balance of organic matter and robotics correct for the creature to live and function properly!" he continued to tell himself as the last bits of the creature had been altered. "This one will work!"

He jolted a bit of electricity into the creature's heart to jump start it once again. The creature's body kicked and flailed as it's no long dead limbs began to spirt back to life, its eyes jutting open and looking around wildly.

The creature surprised Servo though, as it jumped to its feet, slamming hard against the ground as it slipped from them.

"Easy there, easy. You need to adjust." He pleaded to the creature, looking over his shoulder in hopes no one had heard the thing messing about. "You must stay quiet, as what I have done with you should not be exposed yet!"

The creature listened, the cybernetics in its brain translating the speech for it to understand. It sat down, still looking around confused as to what was happening around it.

Servo quickly approached it, inspecting the movement of the body parts one by one and testing the systems he had put in place.

"Everything seems to be working fine for you, try to walk around for me; but slowly."

The creature abided, sliding back to its wobbling feet and attempting a few steps. The creature suddenly stopped after a few, looking around in fright before letting out a ear shattering howl.

Servo looked on in terror as the creatures body began to convulse, sending it to the ground. The electronic components melting directly through the skin. Bits of foam and blood began to poor out of its mouth, nose and eyes as it slammed it body into the ground.

He could not think to react to the creatures suffering, as this was not like the others. The others had all simply fell to the ground.

He rushed over once he could get his mind working properly, but all too late. The creature let out one last painful howl as bits of its own stomach poured from its mouth and onto the ground. He sat there staring at it for a few moments to gather his emotions before turning back to his databoard, working on the new schematics for the cyborg, quickly erasing the last experiment labeled "Leot" from the history.

*   *   *

Sotron has watched the views of the bots hundreds of times, examining every bit of the town they had discovered. He recognized several human artifacts, even some seemingly fresh food scattered throughout the village, many of which went unnoticed by the bot who had seen them in the first place.

"Humans?" he asked himself, shaking the feeling off rather quickly. "No they were all destroyed in the wars, maybe some cluster of robots or other sentient life."

A few of the bots he had appointed as officers came into the command room, each of the pausing at the door with a slight bow before entering.

"Sir, we found the location of the cave, it's just outside of here." The bot pointed directly at the coordinates of one of the Birthed outposts. "Nothing remains in the cave, most of it collapsed from the explosions from within."

"Orotho?" Sorton whispered, examining the coordinates.

"That's not all sir, we found…something buried close to the cave entrance. It was marked with some odd stones with odd engravings on them." The bot continued, a few new images from his own head now showing on the screen.

"Here lies Misfit, reaching his true escape" Sorton read, tilting his head slightly in confusions. "This is a grave marker like the humans had done." He thought to himself.

He quickly scrolled around through the images. This one named "Misfit" was buried about 7 feet into the ground, recently at the. It had the look of something that was once human but became more machine than man.

"Cyborgs?!" Sorton exclaimed, the human foods and items suddenly coming back to mind from the cave. "How many of these graves did you find? Where they all like this? Did you find any alive?" Sorton was beginning to lose his patients.

"We found more than 50 sir, one of them was still partly uncovered, the remains of one of these Cyborgs still holding the shovel found torn mostly to shreds by something in the hole." The bot shoved an image of gore and machinery onto the screen.

Sorton sighed a little in relief. "Then that colony of Cyborgs has been destroyed." He turned away from the screen to face the bots in the room, their glowing red eyes staring directly at him.

"We have more news sir." The bot continued. "It seems that the outpost Orotho has only a handful of guards protecting one of Johnny's higher functioning droids. One of the scouts we caught in the field showed excess memories of him as the one who helped design the Birthed soldiers."

Sorton nodded, attempting to hide his excitement. "Then you have your orders, take the base, preserve the droid and bring him here for re-birthing."

The bots did not hesitate, bowing slightly before heading out of the room. Sorton was alone once more, something he found he preferred in these situations. "Why would Johnny send his droid to Orotho of all places?"

*   *   *

Jared watched the horizon as a few storm clouds began to form over the remnants of a human city. He fought to keep himself focused on his task the Servo had assigned him, aiming down his scope once more, scanning the horizon for a rad-wolf or any other larger rad animal. Nothing had been seen for more than 5 hours of the such.

He needed to get the animal though, as Servo had the authority to destroy him and the others on a whim.

"Fucking nutbag." He thought to himself many times when dealing with Servo.

He and the other bots in the outpost knew what he was doing with the animals, attempting to make some abomination of a robot. They said nothing though. They knew if he caught wind of them attempting to "rat" him out to the others they themselves would be scrapped and mixed with his experiments.

Jared went against regulation, jumping over the ledge and out into the wastes, leaving his laz-rifle behind in favor of his hand shini. He ran out into the wastes, looking for an animal of any kind to appease the psychotic Servo.

He darted in and out of different caves, he assumed were made to help protect from the rains, finding nothing any of them aside from old bones and dried blood from their kills. This was the case more than 4 times before something interesting came to his attention. On the 7th cave he found fresh remnants of fighting of some kind, both scratches and bullet holes littering the floor and walls. There was no bodies though, no robotic remnants often found after a rad-animal found the bot had no flesh. Nothing.

Something gleaned from the light outside, casting a small spot light into the cave for a split second before disappearing.

Jared turned his attention to the entrance, his blue eyes illuminating dimly on the walls. Nothing to be seen. He shook it off, wanting nothing more than to get back to his quarters to do nothing as he so loved to do.

He pushed himself back out of the cave, intentionally ignoring the humanoid footprints in the dirt. He continued back to Orotho, calling the mission a bust. He walked no more than 20 paces before something slammed silently against his shoulder. He fell to the ground, feeling the electricity flowing through him, his systems shutting down one by one before his mind went blank.

*   *   *

Johnny watched as the call out to Servo once again failed. He tapped his fingers against the console in front of him, the random typing and whirring of the machines around him the only sounds. He once more peeked over to the Doppler system, watching as the heavy storm front moved over Orotho.

"He's alright, the storm is just interfering with the com systems." He told himself as he turned back to the reason he was calling Servo.

A small, newer model of scout lay on an examination table somewhere else in Jaxfell,, broadcast to him through camera systems. Lying beside the bot was some form of rad animal, though unlike the others this one nuzzled against the scout, trying to wake it up.

He watched as the beast wrapped one of its 6 greenish arms around the scout and closed its eyes to sleep.

"Strange indeed." He thought to himself as he turned his attention back to the scout's findings, most of which being mutated plants and small dead non-rad animals that seemed fresh.

"At least they found signs of life, a good sign before the war. Now what will become of them if this war grows to the point of the human wars?" his mind flashed back to the explosions that raked the earth while he hid in the bunker.

* * *

Brit lay on the table, her motor and speech functions still not operational. The warning indicator in her vision showing major damage to parts of her body from overheating and electrical damage. She was also keenly aware of her new friend staying by her side, growling at any of the bots that came near her.

"I would have never thought a rad animal would have saved me." She thought as she strained to adjust her vision to look at the arm that had been wrapped around her. "I do hope they do not attempt to do anything to him."

The repair droids had been coming in and out, switching out components in her body to no avail, leading to the only thing that could be the cause as her processing unit itself not able to force the functions. A wave of sadness had been waiving over her knowing they would have to transfer her memories to a new body, though from what she had heard those bots did not seem themselves afterwards; almost devoid of emotions.

"I cannot allow me to be lost!" She angrily thought, sending all of her ability to simply move her arm, a processing overload warning filling her vision. She did not care though, as she knew she needed to move or else the transfer would be the only choice.

A few seconds past as she tried with all of her ability to move her arm, managing only to twitch a few fingers. Her new friend noticed, incessantly pushing against the arm she was trying to move. Her arm moved slightly, though she could not tell if it was from the beast of her own efforts. She tried once more, managing a few inches without the beast before the arm fell back to the table.

She tried to turn her head to look Trunder, only managing a few centimeters of movement. Trunder looked her directly in the eyes, a few tears forming in his eyes as he nuzzled her and whimpered.

"I'm…okay….Trunder." She managed to force out, her system warnings now beginning to turn off a few of her systems indefinitely.

Trunder did not stop though, continuing to push again her. Her arm lay limp, her sensors for it now gone, her systems unable to even read it was there.

One of the service droids drifted into the room, rushing over to her with an odd looking device. Something about the droid looked odd to her, though she could not place her fingers on what. She watched as it passed by her body and out of site. Trunder did not flinch at the bot, continuing to attempt to get her to move.

A jolt shocked her, sending her body into an instant sitting position, Trunder jumping in fright.

Her systems detected a large portion of data flowing into her body and mind, her consciousness fighting against most of it. Most of the data reflected that of her own, but some bits were different. Her memory program began to lose files about the leaders Jax and Johnny, quickly being replaced by new ones. Her xerophia light began to shift from blue to red. Before anything else could happen, a few bots burst through the door, opening fire directly at the bot, sending it to pieces of burning metal.

The device attached to her fell out with the droids burning arm. The light turning back from red to blue. Trunder growled and barked at the bots in the room, jumping between her and them.

They paid him no mind, nor her. A second droid rushed in, plugging in his own device to her.

Her files started to go back to normal, though she did copy the new ones over to a new system, drifting them to her own databoard. The droid was only there for a few seconds before nodding at the camera on the ceiling and leaving the room with the other bots.

Trunder lay next to her, placing his head in her lap and looking up at her. She pet him, eyes never leaving the camera on the ceiling. She made a mental note to check those files they had wished to dispense of so quickly.

* * *

Jared awoke where he had fallen. He stood quickly, weapon drawn as he looked around him. A storm has formed overhead, the clouds threatening him with acid as he stared. He had no time to think, he rushed to Orotho as fast as he possible could. His systems screamed at him as the joints began to overheat from the friction.

The outpost welcomed him in with no hesitation or questions, the dome letting him through with no access request needed.

He had only been in for a few moments before the rain poured down in blankets. The dome above sizzling and screeching with every drop. He was thankful to be back in, vowing to never leave again.

After a few more moments to allow his joints to cool, he inspecting where he had been struck just before his systems rebooted.

A strange clamping device had broken through the metal of his external armor systems and hooked with what seemed like fish hooks snapped into his wiring. The back of the device seemed to at one point to have been attached to some form of cable, no doubt to send electricity to the device.

He took the device off as fast as he could, inspecting it in his hands. Servo quickly approached him, breaking his concentration on the alien device.

"Where have you been? Where are my specimens?" He asked, firing question after question that Jared simply blocked out. Instead he slammed the device against Servo's head and walked away.

"A shocker hook?!" He could here Servo exclaim before stepping into his own quarters. He sat at his recharge station, a few small ant droids Servo had developed flowed down to the wound, welding it back together.

*   *   *

Mikeli marched in the shadows towards their target. Orotho sat just close to 34 minutes away from them, the storm forcing them into a few underground cave systems. They blasted at a few of the rad-animals that came at them. Their red lights no doubt drawing the attention of everything in the darkness.

They headed forward, the mission to avenge their brethren the only thing on their mind. There were 4 others in this cave with him, though more than 40 in total in the system towards Orotho. Each of them built the same, long narrow legs, light armor, dimmer caps on their red glowing eyes, and small sensor blockers attached to their heads.

"Assassin model" branded on the arms just beneath their insignia of Rebirthed. Built for speed and stealth, favoring close range hand to hand weaponry over the fire arms, though each had a blaster.

Mikeli moved ahead of the rest, acting as leader for the group. 15 minutes to Orotho.

Something he did not expect to happen sent him flying. Gunfire burst through the cave, catching him and the others off guard. No lights from xerophia shined through the darkness other than their own. He fired a few return shots, broadcasting to the others in the system for reinforcements. No response.

A few bullets plowed through them like the humans old paper. Mikeli sat in silence, covering the xerophia light with a bit of dirt to cover the light. The other bots he was with fell, their lights going off permanently.

Something moved in the dark in front of him, though he could not see what. A sudden light filled his vision, doing what he could to not react to it. The light went off as quickly as it came, and footsteps away from him grew quiet.

He silently sat there, not knowing how long it would be. Nor what he had just seen.

* * *

Servo worked furiously on the electro hook, not hearing of the devise being used since the human wars against bots. He had uncovered many things about it, one of which being that it was a reproduction made of lesser materials.

After his examination of the device he sat thinking for a while.

"Who built this? The rebirthed make their mark on the devices the make, as do we. Yet this has a different insignia." He thought, examining the odd insignia of a humanoid eye with a blade through it. "Further why would they attack but not kill?"

He shook his head before returning to his latest experiment, a rad wolf with 6 legs and greenish fir. He had replaced 2 of its legs with metal legs, as well as half of its brain. He even sprayed just beneath the fir some bits of metal armoring.

Before he could switch thee creature on, the alarms sounded for an attack.

*   *   *

Jared rushed to his post, his new shini aimed at the ready. Somehow the attackers disabled the energy dome, something no one has been able to do.

He aimed out into the wastes, looking for what was coming in at them, no signs of movement. The alarm continued to blare behind him, repeating the same high pitch siren second after second.

He lowered his arms, confusion filling him.

"What the fu.." he did not get to finish what he was saying. An explosion racked the outpost, bits of metal and concrete flying around from the explosion. Dust billowed into the air, surrounding every last bit of what he could see.

Gunfire flew from out of the clouds of dust. Catching Jared off guard. He returned fire, going full out into the cloud. Unsure of what was firing at him or if he was even hitting the targets.

A few shoti blast fired out, one catching Jared in the leg, sending it flying back and him to the floor. He continued firing, his mind racing knowing this could be his last moments. Another shoti blast lurched out just in front of his face, smashing into his head. It took out most of it, sending his systems into shut down. As his mind started to go blank he thought to himself.

"But nothing happens in Orotho."

*   *   *

Servo rushed out of his room, heading towards the bunker further in for protection. Gunfire had already reached inside of the building. A mix of blasters, shinis, shotis, and lazers firing echoed close by. He went into overdrive, sending himself down the hallway towards the bunker. A few odd shadows followed close behind him. He fired a few shots from his hand blaster back at them, never looking back.

A turn to the left, a turn to the right, and he was at the bunker. The door was already locked closed. He banged on the door with all of his might, knowing full well that it would not be heard from inside the bunker. He quickly turned around to see his attackers. A rad lion popped around the corner slowly, but it was no normal rad lion.

One of the lion's eyes was robotic, glaring with a purple coloring directly at him. 2 of its 4 legs where mechanical in nature, bits of fake flesh dripping from in slightly. Mounted to its back was a large old gatling gun, something that had not been seen even since before the war had started outside of museums.

"It's so beautiful!" He exclaimed as the gatling gun whirred to life, sending a salvo of bullets directly into him, splattering metal and coolant everywhere. "If only I could have made it!" he thought as his systems shut down and his consciousness faded away permanently.

Chapter 8 – A New Menace.

Johnny sat looking at the storm dissipating as well as the scout bot, Brit her name he was told, and her new pet.

"He is going to have to see this, maybe run some tests on her systems and its brain. We need to find why the wolf took to her and she did not kill it on site." He thought to himself.

He hailed out to Orotho as the last of the storm left the area. "You better answer." He thought to himself as the transmission was connecting for the call.

"Who are you?" a voice echoed out to him, one not of a machine he had heard before.

Johnny sat silent, watching the flashing video error on the console.

"Who are you?" the voice asked once more, this time a bit more aggression behind the tone.

"I am Johnny, leader of the Birthed bots, and founder of Jaxfell. Who are you to ask me who I am?" He replied, not even attempting to hide his anger, the realization of Servo more than likely being destroyed coming to mind.

"We are the Survivors!" The voice replied, ending the transmission.

Johnny sat, body shaking slightly with anger, knowing now full well Orotho was lost. Confusion did come into play though, as he did not know what had taken it.

"That was no bot." he told himself as he sat straight, clicking a few selections on the console. 5 new bots appeared on screen, each a leader of a different town or outpost.

"We need soldiers from you all, something has taken Orotho, and we need to get it back from them." He sternly shouted at them.

"It's only Orotho sir, there is nothing there worth taking." One of them chimed in at him.

Johnny quickly slammed his fist on the console, causing the image to shimmer and the bots to jump.

"It's not the outpost I am worried about. Something attacked us, possibly destroying or capturing the droid Servo. I sent him there for some research purposes, though he may not have known it. We need to find if he is lost, recover his memories, or recover him." Johnny sat for a second, waiting for any kind of reply from the bots.

The other sat in silence for a few long seconds before all nodded. "Our soldiers are yours." One said, before clicking off the screen. The others following suit shortly after.

"We will take him back, and destroy those who oppose us." Johnny whispered before heading back to his quarters for his vice.

*   *   *

Brit sat in her new quarters, Trunder laying down by her feet sound asleep. She had been looking through the files she had copied, hiding them from the droids that occasionally came to check on her.

She had been placed here on restriction until they could be ensured no true damage had been done to her. She did not mind it much, though she did miss the wastes where she felt the most comfortable.

Through her exploring the files she had discovered why they wanted to keep her under close watch. Much of it was simple history files, though their validity she could not tell. Some of them logs from the bot Kerith labeled his adventure log.

Other files seemed to be hacking programs, though no data transfer was in them. It seemed the program was meant to take down some program in her systems she could not even detect was in her. This, of all things, worried her.

"What is the program that it is trying to take down used for?" She asked herself multiple times, an answer never coming to mind.

A few droids came in for inspection and check up on her. She sat with them, doing her best to sit still for them. A thought came to mind.

"What is the FHL program?" She asked the droid checking her programming. The droid, not expecting the question stepped back, unhooking his devices from her.

"It is the base program for your knowledge and memories." The bot responded hastily.

"He's lying." She thought to herself.

"Why do you ask?" the droid quickly plugging the devices in once more, now inspecting her memory files.

"When the enemy started reprogramming me, it was trying to remove it is all. I had never heard of it and scanning my systems I cannot find it." She lied, hoping it would distract the droid enough to fool it.

"'No worries, the program is still intact, or else you wouldn't be able to remember the attack in the first place." The droid said, finishing his scan and removing the devices once more. "All systems green, just a while longer and back to the wastes you go."

The droid and his repair droid friend left the room, glancing back as the left.

"There is something more going on here than they want me to know." She thought to herself, petting Trunder gently as the droids had stirred him. She grabbed a few pieces of meat from the newly installed refrigeration unit and fed them to Trunder. "We will get to the bottom of it."

*   *   *

Sorton sat listening to the bots story of monsters in the dark, with glowing white eyes in the darkness of the caves.

"All of this in the underground caverns by Orotho?" He asked the bot one more time.

"Yes, we took shelter there during the storms to save ourselves and sneak past their defenses." The bot replied, anger now filling his voice after repeating the story for the 4th time.

Sorton nodded as he began to pace back and forth. He had a new mystery on his hands.

"First an entire squad of bots destroyed by an explosion in a cavern filled with old human relics, now a battalion of bots destroyed in caverns closer to

Orotho." He thought to himself, the bot looking at him following is every step. "All except this one, nothing that has encountered the things living in the caves and caverns have lived. Has Johnny gotten that wise?"

He shook it quickly off, turning his attention quickly back to the bot before him.

"You will return to Orotho, this time do not enter the caverns. Scout it out and see what you can find there." Sorton quickly waved his hand to send off the bot. The bot without a word bowed and left the room.

Sorton sat at the console for communication over the radio waves, a primitive system but one they found the Birthed could not receive. He selected a few different options on the screens, a static sound coming over the speaker next to it.

"Attention all bots in the field, we may have a new enemy entering the fray. Keep your guard up, we cannot allow them to stop our mission to bring the truth to all bots, and free them from the control they are enslaved to!" He announced, shutting off the system once finished.

He had sent more than 300 bots out into the wastes, taking over close to 14 outposts and 2 small towns from the Birthed. Even in taking down the cities with newer more advanced weapons than his own army's, he had only lost a hand full of bots. To this new threat he had lost more than triple that.

"Whatever has been taking out our bots, we must stop it." He thought to himself, turning back once more to his console to continue working on his new creations.

*　　　　　*　　　　　*

Mikeli crawled through what he hopes was grass towards the hill front close to Orotho. He had his sniper lazer clenched close to his chest as he crawled, keeping keenly aware for any movement or sound around him. He reached the top of the hill, the grass still thick around him. With a quick flick, his weapon was aimed and ready. He connected the end of the scope to his facial jack, his vision quickly switching to the weapons scope.

What he saw, his mind could not recognize. Some form of organic beings walked around in the walls, closing up what seemed to be a large hole in the center of the outpost. He zoomed in more to get a better look at what was not controlling the outpost.

After a couple of quick zoom changes he could see things a bit more clearly through the scope. The organic creature seemed to be some form of large cat, a large gatling gun strapped to its back, 2 of its legs replaced with mechanical robotic legs, as well as one of its eyes. He switched view to another of the organic creatures, confusion beginning to fill him.

The second one seemed bipedal, almost human. The only concerning factor was the head was fully robotic, the rest being a greyish flesh covered in a few bits of cloth and metal. This one was shoveling dirt back into the hole. A few more bipedal beings where helping him, each one having different portions replaced with robotic parts, though all of the heads where at least partially mechanical in nature.

An odd looking robot wondered around them, a fake smile painted on its face, with a purple energy glowing from its xerophia pod and mismatched eyes. The top of its head had a bit of that same flesh as the others, held on by a purple band.

"Cyborgs?!" he gasped, quickly sliding himself down the hill and unplugging the scope in one quick motion. "I need to get back now!" he thought as he switched from a walk to a full sprint.

He made it nearly a quarter of the way back to base when something struck his shoulder and every system in his body shut down.

* * *

William looked down at his capture, admiring the new weaponry that came with the bot. The red eyes glowing faintly as the system power kept it alive. He snapped the electro cable as he grabbed the bot and proceeded to push it away.

The bot lay motionless. As he proceeded to scavenge for weapons and ammunition, discarding the things that where not useful.

"I wonder if they dream." He thought to himself as he slid the items into his pack hanging from his back with his mechanical arm.

He had never quite gotten used to his new mechanical arm or legs, though the mechanical enhancement of his brain did help ease the use. He continued to think as he always had back to when the humans where still around.

He slammed the bot across his back, the spine enhancers taking the brunt of the weight.

"We'll get back to that someday!" he thought to himself as he moved back to Orotho, a smile crossing his face. "Then things will be better."

He stepped back through the gates at Orotho, slamming the bot down to the ground.

"Got one them red ones, spying on us. Old sally here" he lifted his hook gun "took care of that."

A few of the other cyborgs approached the new bot, already trying to salvage the body parts.

"He aint dead yet fools!" William shouted swinging at them with sally. "Boss mans' gonna wanna see em!"

The other cyborgs just went back to what they were doing, some filling the hole while others played guard duty. William dragged the bot behind him as he walked into the outpost's main building, a few cyborgs sweeping up the remains of the bots from the battle. A few turns down a few short corridors later and he was in the command room.

William bowed slightly as he pushed the bot into the center of the room.

"Got one them spies for you. He saw everything, 'as gonna tell them other red ones!" William said, never lifting his head back up.

A four legged little bot came over and jammed a large spike directly into the bots head, the lights going out almost instantly from its eyes and chest. A faint laughter filled the room, sending shivers down William's spine.

"That's a good boy!" A half chuckling voice said quietly from somewhere in the room, a large cat entering William's vision and taking the bot's body away. "Was there anymore William? Anymore toys to play with?!?"

William shook his head "No sir, only the one; but we know were de' be headin'" he replied, trying his best to not look at his commander.

He did not keep that for long as something pushed his head back up to glair directly into painted on crooked teeth and miss matched glowing purple eyes.

"You will bring me more play things yes? So much to be done, so many more toys to make and break" The twisted cyborg said, a cackle in every word.

"Yes Tinker" he whispered under his trembling breath.

"Good good, fun fun." Tinker replied letting go of William's head. "Now go go, I need to work with my new toy!" He said quietly as he turned to the new bot, a saw appearing out of what seemed like nowhere.\

William turned and walked away as the saw revved up and began cutting into the metal, sparks lighting the corridor up.

"Gives me the creeps" he thought to himself as he shivered while walking back out into the daylight.

Chapter 9- Act of Treason

Brit looked over her files, confusion still filling her with every read.

"A false history? Lies of our leader Jax?" She thought to herself, Trunder staring at the door to give warning before any other bots could enter.

She had been reading the information piece by peace and comparing it to her own for a while now, none of it making sense in comparison to the each other. She put them away once more, slipping the databoard into the bag on her left shoulder, hiding it inside a secret pocket she had crafted.

Trunder did a slight growl as a new bot entered, her first reaction to ignore it as it entered.

"Are you eager to get back to your exploring?" Johnny's voice echoed through the room, causing her to jump from her seat.

"Yes sir, I am. I am best in the wastes." She replied, looking directly at the aged bot who oversaw their lives.

Johnny chuckled to himself slightly. "We'll you are most needed in the wastes. Your specimens of plants and animals have improved our work here greatly." He patter her shoulder, her mind fighting the urge to shove it off. "Take your friend here" He looked at Trunder who snarled back at him " to the wastes with you, scanning your memories he is the reason you are still with us here today."

Johnny let go of her and began to walk out of the room but pause.

"Oh, and we will be sending you out with a new databoard and weapon to use in the field." He turned back to look at her. "Your weapon was lost, and the databoard you carry with you may have been damaged as well. We can't have our best scout lost in the field now can we?" and walked out of the room.

Brit fell back to her chair, Trunder rushing over to comfort her.

She did not like the way he had said that to her. "Something is wrong here." She thought to herself, looking at her bag as sneakily as she could. "He may know I have this data, and doesn't want me to." She pet Trunder, handing him a bit of cloned beef with the bone still in it to his delight. "I need to be careful." She thought as Trunder ripped into the meat without hesitation.

*   *   *

Sorton looked over the video footage from the scope had installed on the rifle had had given to the now departed bot. Watching as the cyborgs had entered the battle for earth.

"Why after of all these years do they attack us now?" he asked himself watching the footage once more. "How have they survived?"

There were too many questions that had no logical answers for him, and he did not like it one bit. He watched another monitor as his armies moved in on Orotho, more than 400 strong.

"We will destroy them none the less!" He thought to himself as he sent the attack order to one of the bots who had a distance com unit attached. "They will fall and nothing will stop us from taking back the lies to expose the truth!"

*   *   *

William watched the night lit horizon from his hiding spot, a few mutated insects gnawed at the long dead flesh on his leg. He shooed them away with a quick motion of his hand, the things ripping at the flesh with a silent tear as they ran.

He was there as Tinker had requested, waiting for any kind of movement his way. The borg gave him the creeps.

He thought back to some of the experiments he had seen the borg do on animals and man alike. During the human wars, he had a field day with the scouts that strayed into is traps. He clenched Shella closer at the thought of the agonizing screams that echoed through those nights.

A snap outside alerted him back to the present, something moving in the darkness just outside his hole. He made no sound, as many footsteps proceeded forward past him, the night masking their motion. He clicked his head slightly, his eyes changing to night vision.

He choked down a gasp as hundreds of bots marched towards the outpost. He did not bring a radio with him, as he had at one time alerted his prey with it as someone hailed him.

He needed to alert the outpost as fast as he could though, knowing no matter what he did, he would be lost. He kissed Shella for the last time as he flew from cover, launching a couple of elctro hooks into the nearby bots, their bodies falling quickly to the ground. He threw the weapon to the ground and snagged a couple of their shini's, firing full burst into the crowd of others, sending nearly 15 of them to the ground.

A few thuds hit his chest, his mechanical body fighting to keep him standing with each thud. He felt a heavy pain as his lung collapsed and began to reflate with blood. He fired a few more shots before the gun went click in his hand, sending about 10 more to the scrapyard.

He dropped to his knees as the only thing keeping him alive now where the enhancements to his heart and brain. Grabbing furiously for another weapon, he found none as his vision started to go dark and he felt the earth give way beneath him.

*   *   *

Tinker worked furiously at his new toy, laughing and giggling with every weld and solder her made. The alarms of attack echoed through the halls, but he couldn't care less as he neared finishing his new toy. The siren had begun to wear on him though, causing anger to fill in his mind.

"Fluffy! Fluffinator!!" He angrily growled, the cat in the room running up to his side and making a small meow. "End whatever is causing this racquet while I finish playing? I do need my silence to make it all perfect!"

Fluffinator looked at him and meowed slightly, turning and running off to the battle that no doubt had started outside.

"One little two little three little wires, connect them together to start some fires." He sang to himself as he melted some wiring together. " four little five little 6 little wires, to bring to life all of my desires."

He continued singing his little song as he worked, trying to drown out the sounds of the sirens. Giggling and cackling occasionally.

*   *   *

Fluffinator did as his master had asked him, running out into the fields of the wastes. A few of the cyborg brothers fighting alongside him. His gatling gun firing a non-stop burst of rounds at the incoming bots, the barrels turning a shade of white from the heat of the dispersing rounds.

One by one they fell, some from hi weapon, others from the other cyborgs. Being a mutated cat cyborg, he had no true thoughts that could be translated to speech short of "kill them all" at this moment.

Shell after shell flew from the dispenser, nearly 1000 count strong piling with light clanks at they fell into one another. In a short to no time, the bot charge had stopped, all on the ground either dead, or slowly turning off.

Fluffinator went to each body, sniffing at them and biting at their circuits, his metal teeth ripping through them with ease.

The battle was not yet over though, as his ears picked up a heavy metal sound somewhere in the distance. A low thud, followed by a high pitch squealing echoed through the air.

Not but 20 yards away an explosion engulfed a few of the cyborgs, their screams lasting only a millisecond before being replaced with a loud his of flames.

Fluffinator ran toward where the shot came from, hoping there was enough ammo left to take whatever made the shot out. A few more thumps echoed out, with explosions somewhere behind Fluffinator going off. Something was now visible in the distance, walking tall on 4 large spider like legs. 2 cannons positioned on its top almost like it eyes. A thump came from it as a blue light exploded out. The blast was just short of Fluffinator, some of the fire singeing his fur.

He could feel the energy emitted from the blast messing with his electronics, though he could not understand what was happening to them. All he knew what this device needed to be destroyed for the battle to be over. He ran straight at it, his legs having trouble keeping up the pace as the metal ones began to lock up.

He let out a large salvo of bullets into the device, watching as small holes punched through its shell with ease riddling it with the emp shells. To no avail though, as the device continued moving towards Fluffinator, a small whole opening beneath its cylinder body revealing a small set of blasters. These blasters began to shoot as fast as they could at

Fluffinator, crackles of energy filling his ears with every close shot.

He threw himself left and right, serpentining to avoid the shots, his own cannon never stopping firing. A few of his shells ripped through a couple of the blasters, causing them to overload and form small explosions around them melting the metal of the shell the held them. He was now within touching reach of the device, able to see more clearly it weak points.

A large red xerophia pod sat just on its back, slowly overheating from the loss of coolant. The bullet holes he had riddled the device with leaked coolant like waterfalls, the device fighting to stay standing now.

He let one last salvo out, running his weapon dry as the pod cracked from the shots. He had little understanding of what happened as the device began to spasm. Fear lead him to run back to Orotho, looking back at the device while it fell and kicked like a dying animal. A red explosion wracked the ground around it, sending shockwaves for nearly 40 meters.

The device was destroyed, and hundreds of bodies of bots littered the grounds between him and Orotho. A few cyborgs had already begun to scavenge the dead bots for useful items. Fluffinator did not bother with the bodies, as he needed his master to tend to him. Each step sending bits of pain through his body. Somewhere in that fight something had struck him, bits of blood beginning to leak from the wound.

He limped into the command room, hearing Tinker singing his little songs as he worked.

*   *   *

Johnny watched Brit's movements on his databoard, admiring his genius of placing trackers and cameras on the new weapon and databoard she had received.

"We will find what you do and where you go little miss, and find if they truly did corrupt you." He said quietly to the screen as one of the blaster bots he had sent for came into the room, bowing a few times before stating his business.

"Sir you asked for me?" The bot asked, never dropping his at attention stance.

Johnny looked at the bot examining him closely. He noticed no damages to the bot.

"I sent for you, and all of your squad. Yet only you arrive?" Johnny placed the databoard down on the command console. "So tell me, where the others destroyed on the mission at Orotho? Why do you return with no damage or word of victory?" He hammered at the bot. "Why? Speak up!"

"We had orders of retreat back to Jaxfell, broadcast to us directly from you. In good time as well, as hundreds of bots marched to Orotho." The bot replied. He stood for a second before presenting his own databoard. "Here is the video of the events and audio of the retreat order if you would like sir."

Johnny paused for a second, looking down at the databoard. "Did I call for retreat?" he asked himself as he grabbed the databoard. He could not remember sending an order for retreat to the bots, and needed proof of it.

He sat and watched the video, listening closely to the audio, hearing his own voice request a return to Jaxfell. Something was wrong with it though, it had a static element to it. Almost as if it was one of the radio manipulators from the human war. He saw the hundreds of red glowing lights in the darkness just passed the cover the bot before him had taken, also seeing what looked like a cyborg fly from the darkness and beginning to destroy the bots one by one.

"Cyborgs?!" Johnny exclaimed looking back at the blaster bot. "So it's true then?"

The bot nodded gently. "Yes, we saw the cyborg attacking. We have reason to believe these cyborgs are the Survivors that took Orotho." He replied, his one large eye never losing contact with Johnny's.

Johnny nodded, the anger still boiling just beneath the surface. He had to think quickly of what to do next, for if they had the ability to imitate hit voice through short wave signals, than nothing could stop them from providing false orders.

"Gather your men, gather all that are available for battle in Jaxfell. Take 3 spider tanks with you, we go to take back Orotho from these Survivors and end them like we should have in the human wars." He replied to the bot turning back to his console, body shaking from the stress. "We send you to either your doom or theirs!"

The bot must have left when he wasn't looked for when he turned around no-one was there.

"Curse you Jax" he thought to himself. "If you only had shared the warp knowledge during the war, we would not have any of these concerns."

He sighed to himself before turning back to the creation that had been brought to him. "It is time for you to come into play now" He said as he pressed the engage on their manufacturing.

*   *   *

Sorton slammed his fist over and over into the wall next to him, shattering both the wall and his hand in the process. The bots standing before him took a few steps back as the bot began to lose control of his anger.

"Jax forsaken cyborgs." He shouted to himself, slamming his hand one last time against the wall, snapping it off at the wrist. "They took out everything we could send at them!" He looked over at the other bots. "Send in the Kamikaze units!" He shouted throwing a handful of wall at them, his broken hand flying with it.

The bots did not hesitate in the slightest, each running off to gather the Kamikaze units.

Sorton looked over at a progress bar on the console. Fenrir was almost ready for his use, he just needed more time.

"We must not let them have this battle, or any other." He shouted at the screen, his body alarming him of the broken hand.

*   *   *

Brit wondered close to the remains of a battle that must have been fresh, body parts of the fallen still shrouding the wastes. She looked around for any movement, but nothing. She checked her location on the databoard, showing the nearest outpost as Orotho.

Having been in the field for a few days now, she thought it best to get a coolant change while she could, moving a few steps in that direction. She noticed something odd about the location on the map, as Orotho glowed a purple color instead of its normal blue.

She paid it no mind as she headed over, her coolant rate at 35%. Trunder by her side seemed on edge, no doubt smelling something in the air she could not detect. She paused as Orotho came into view, no movement from its inside, no guards positioned at its walls. Nothing.

She quickly slid against a few of the dead Rebirthed that had been piled up, a light ting as the metal collided with one another.

She slid out a view magnified from her bag on her left, sliding it over her right eye. She gasped at what she saw.

"Cyborgs?!" she coughed out as the vision of a few of the dead just outside the walls filled her right eyes vision. She quickly scouted her vision around the area looking for any signs of bots or borgs moving. Nothing showed.

She readied her weapon as she slid the magnifier back into her bag, nodding at Trunder who positioned himself just beside her.

She climbed atop him, keeping her head low and weapon aimed straight ahead. With no warning Trunder took to full speed, hammering at over 60 mph towards the quickly approaching walls. No alarms went off as they flew through the walls,

Trunder skidding to a halt. Brit Rolled off, quickly re-aiming her weapon at eye level. Nothing.

She ran full speed, Trunder just behind her, to the command building. The door opened without being prompted as she flew through it, Trunder not missing a beat. She slid against the wall of a corridor, Trunder Slamming into a few rooms around them.

She could hear a faint laughter from somewhere down the hall, something she did not expect to hear. She crept towards it Trunder focusing with her on the source of the laughter in the dark. A few turns later and they were just outside of the command room, the laughter almost unbearably loud now.

Brit kicked at the door gently to trigger its auto open, the doors opening quicker than she expected. She had no time to truly react to the Cyborgs grabbing at her, managing only a few shout into one's head, sending it slumping to the ground. Trunder barked and snarled furiously as he attacked, snapping at their necks and arms for the kill. He manager to rip one's head clean off before something flew from the crowd and struck him with a loud thud followed quickly by a yelp and whimper as Trunder fell unconscious.

Brit found herself un-armed and dragged into the center of the room. Trunder was dragged in with her, his body not moving aside from the occasional breath.

She was thrown down, the laughter now ear piercing, the borg who it emitted from pointing at an area sensor with laughter, brits image flashing over the screens.

"Puppy whuppy, and missy sissy fell into the spider's web, never knowing what they see." The laughing one chuckled, never looking back at them. "The spiders not hungry though, so instead he wants to play." The bot turned around, the false painted smile and blazing purple mismatched eyes glaring at her. "Now missy sissy and puppy whuppy wish they had stayed on their tuffit."

He laughed even louder now. Something moved out of the corner of her eye, drawing her attention.

What looked like one of Johnny's droids stumbled into the center of the room past the cyborgs. Something was off about it, as large arachnid legs supported its body instead of its normal humanoid legs. A few bullet holes riddled its chest and head, but its eyes still glowed and functioned.

"A simple wasteland scout? How quaint!" it spoke at her, examining her body closely. "Standard armor, standard female body style, all average." He scoffed and turned to Trunder. "A rad wolf, well fed, good strength." He paused for a moment and turned back to Brit. "A wasteland scout befriended a rad animal without being torn to shreds? Inconceivable!" The droid turned back quickly and rushed past the cyborgs muttering to himself under his breath. Brit was only able to discern a few lines, one of which being "experiments need to be done on them".

The cackling one stopped laughing suddenly and jumped forward at her with no warning, causing her to jump in fear.

"Missy sissy little girl, all alone in this dark dark world. Only puppy whuppy by her side; but soon so soon they will share their insides!" He sang at her laughing directly in her face before something struck the back of her head, sending shocking through her whole body and shutting her systems down. The painted grin was the last thing she saw before her systems shut down.

*   *   *

Johnny watched as the scout passed out from the electro hook. His body began to shake as he clenched his fists.

"Servo, you betray us for these sick experiments?!" He shouted at the screen. The Survivors now crowded around her a few laughing with the cackling one. One of the borgs looked directly into the scope of the new weapon and laughed into the camera before smashing it.

Johnny looked over his shoulder at one of the droids who was watching with him. The droid looked back at him and then back to the screen.

"Traitors must be dealt with!" The droid chimed in, turning back to his work. "Shall we launch the counter attack now sir?"

Johnny sat thinking for a few moments, as he had already gathered to forces with the bots he had sent for.

"Send the orders, and launch our new creations with them!" Johnny shouted, standing with lightning speed, his metal feet sparking on the metallic floor. "I want them destroyed! All of them!"

Johnny rushed back to his room, his body beginning to shake as he sat in the same old coolant station.

"Just one last time" He said as once more he began to overload his systems with the electricity as he had so often done.

*   *   *

Josh sat on his assigned Kamikaze unit, the ground around him flying by like a blur. He and the 13 others had set off no more than 2 hours prior and they found themselves not but a day's ride to the Orotho outpost.

He laughed to himself as the rad animals they passed seemed frightened by the quick movement. The laughter was his own way of coping with the knowledge they rode to their destruction.

He thought back on his ride to when he was first built, his own dreams being quickly dispatched to be replaced with the mission of destroying the Birthed and these cyborgs.

"I had wanted to be a biological experimenter." He thought to himself as the unit beneath him bounced on the rough terrain. "How ironic that we fight for freedom and truth to all bots, yet we ourselves are not free."

He had many thoughts like that on this ride. He knew what he was doing was for the betterment of the robotic race; but simply wished he could have the chance to do what he dreamt of.

*   *   *

Crystal marched with the other bots that had been sent to Orotho. She looked down at her shini and sighed as she marched. The spider tank moved just behind her with loud thuds as it walked, thee tanks slowing their progress by more than half a day.

She was glad she was not one of the lower blaster bots, as many of them where tasked with carrying the new twisted droid creations. Each one seemed to be a pill shaped capsule, though none of them quiet knew what lay inside.

She had been curious when they started what the capsules could be hiding, though she had not looked as she had been ordered not to.

"Why did he put a blaster bot in charge of us?" she asked herself as she watched their commanding bot ride the back of one of the spider tanks. "Why not a shini bot? Further, why not send us in those sky birds?"

These questions ate at her, as the mission seemed to be a futile effort to take out the Survivors and retrieve the useless Orotho.

She had, before being gathered for this battle, been set as a guard in Cogsmin. She did miss Cogsmin dearly as the archaic technology fascinated her, all the doors and items in the city powered by cogs that span from the running underground springs.

None the less she intended to get back to her home there.

The walk was nearly finished, Orotho resting only about 1 mile from them. The blaster bot stopped the group, jumping down from his spider tank. He walked to each of the pills the other blasters carried and slammed them into the ground.

Once the capsules touched the ground, clamping hands flew from their bottoms, implanting themselves beneath the dirt. The tops popped open extending out to show a small robotic head with a single eye. Beneath the head an array of electronics and barrels pointed out in front of it. Each barrel lead to a hidden weapon inside its body, each one shaped different.

Crystal looked at the thing in confusion, as it seemed more of a turret than an attacking weapon. She did not have time to think on it to long as a few of the spider cannons fired at the outpost, a mixture of plasma blasts and emp shells flying at it with earth bending speed.

A few of the shells made contact with the wall as the shots fell short, while other slammed into the side of the command building. Some of the walls burst while other melted away from the white hot plasma.

A large number of enemies piled out of the building, firing blindly at the direction of the spider tanks. A few stray shots clipped a few of the Birthed bots around Crystal, sending theirs bodies flying as bits of their metal sparked and scattered into the field.

The tanks continued firing behind them, the barrels turning a shade of blue from the heat, bits of the metal beginning to melt from it. One of the borgs in the distance propelled itself at them at alarming speeds. The tanks tried to keep up with the approaching threat, but its speed was far too great. The turrets began to spin to life, aiming all their barrels at the oncoming threat. Bursts of fire emerged from the barrels, a mix of emp shots, plasma, lazer, and rockets flew from them at rapid succession. The air around them burned with heat, the grass beneath catching fire.

    The enemy dodged every shot, now visible as a large cat with an oversized weapon attached to its back. The bots did not wait to join on the firing. The air filled with the defining roar of hundreds of mixed rounds flying through the air all at once.

    The cat was struck by a few shots, roaring silently in pain at a distance. It did not hesitate to turn back and sprint the other way, the gun on its back turning to face them and firing full auto at them. More than 20 bots fell instantly, their bodies blowing apart into hundreds of bits.

"Explosive rounds!" someone in the carnage shouted as a few of the rounds struck the ground and exploded from the cat. Crystal quickly took cover behind the leg of one of the spider tanks.

The tanks had taken more damage than she had thought, coolant pouring down its leg mixed with bits of metal from the wounds. Crystal looked at the tank she hid beneath, its body shaking to keep itself up as its systems began to overheat.

She ran from the cover as fast as she could, unsure when it would give way. Her attention focused as she ran on the enemies, none seeming to be approaching them. Instead they ran to the hills, slipping into unseen caves and caverns.

The turrets stopped firing almost at once as the last of the enemies slid into the caves. A cheer echoed through the hills.

Crystal looked around at the bots, their number dropping to about 1/3 what they had started with. A sigh passed her by, knowing with this victory she would be able to go back home.

* * *

Josh looked at a distance as the Birthed took over the outpost once more. Watching as the bots stepped into the remains of their once un-needed outpost.

"Go now!" He shouted at the others, the Kamikaze units flying full speed at the Birthed units. He watched the ground fly passed, his weapon aimed straight forward to help ensure the Kamikaze made its mark.

The Birthed spotted them before they could get within range to use their own low end blaster pistols. A few stray shots fired passed him, cutting through the air with a loud whistle as they passed.

One of the bots behind him was stuck, flying to the ground off its Kamikaze unit. The body broke to pieces as it collided with the still standing ground. The remains disappeared somewhere in the distance.

Josh fired a few shots at the crowd of bots they rapidly approached, catching of a few of them in the legs sending them to the ground instantly.

He was struck a few times in the chest by a few shini shots, his arm gripping the Kamikaze unit beneath him to prevent falling off. His systems screamed at him of the damage, a few of his systems already beginning to overheat.

He fired a few more shots as he passed through the gates, catching a few odd capsule looking devices that a few had carried.

He shut off his vision as the wall of the command building approached him rapidly. He thought of the beautiful plants he had wished to make as the Kamikaze unit collided with the building, sending him flying into the walls as the area turned to glass from the explosions.

*   *   *

Crystal was knocked away from the walls as the outpost exploded before her, more than 12 large smoked clouds billowing out of what remained of the walls. A few other bots around her struggled to sit up as the emp blast from a few of the explosions had begun to wreak havoc on their systems.

As the fired began to dissipate, a few cyborgs emerged from a few unseen caverns, laughing wildly as if they knew this was going to happen.

Crystal fell back to the ground, forcefully shutting down her own systems before the borgs could salvage her while she still functioned.

Chapter 10 – Something Lost, Something Gained

Brit's eyes came back, her consciousness lost and confused at being brought back. Her hope were high, looking around for the all too familiar droids. None were to be found.

She instead found herself in what looked like one the wastes underground caverns, with slight differences though. The cave walls a ceiling around her were the same light brown she had come to know from her adventures out into the wastes; but the floor and contents are what confused her.

The cave floor seemed to be made of old pavement, cracked from age, had remnants of humans with long faded lines of paint here and there. The surroundings having rudimentary shacks with bits of furniture poking through some of the windows or doors.

The smell of fresh meat lingered in the air around her. Her stomach beginning to growl with hunger.

This caused a pause. She could smell. She had hunger. All these things new to her. She looked down and found not her own body but a greenish fur looking back at her, some of the individual hairs moving in the wind.

Her mind could barely comprehend what was happening to her, forcing herself to move, feeling the ground beneath her for the first time. The body she had now did not obey the commands as she had asked, sending her sprawling to the ground. She was not keenly aware of having more than 2 or even 4 legs.

A blank realization hit her with a ton of bricks.

"I have Trunder's body now.." she thought looking around furiously.

A small cackling emitted from the cave somewhere, no doubt its source watching her in the dark.

She tried to shout out at them but was only able to emit a loud barking sound. The cackling changed to sheer laughter at that.

"Missy sissy and puppy whuppy now in the same body, sharing the brain and all its pain. So much fun with this toy. Now made one that is both girl and boy." The cackling voice shouted at her.

Brit tried to understand the riddle like rhymes of the mad one.

"So me and Trunder now share a body and mind?" she thought to herself. With all of her mind's ability she now tried to get in touch with Trunder, attempting to visualize a nice well-cooked steak.

That got his attention in a heartbeat, the body moving without her controlling it, their now shared head looking around for the food from her mind.

She was astonished, he was now able to see what images where in her head. She could barely comprehend this, as nothing like this had been done in the time of the robots.

"Food?" she heard in her head, a slightly growled voice creating it.

"Trunder?" she replied in her own mind, the body shaking and looking for something.

"Master?" Trunder asked, the body now spinning around and whimpering. "Where is master?"

Brit tried to think of some way to explain to him where she was. She tried showing him images of their 2 bodies merged when it occurred to her, she did not know what they looked like at all either.

"We are now one"' She tried to tell him simply, hoping that he could understand.

"How do I hear you? How do you know what I am thinking? How can I move without wanting to?" He started firing multiple questions at her, now knowing she could understand him.

The cackling one came into view, his false painted smile mocking her. The body emitted a growl at him.

"Puppy whuppy play nice, or punishment for you!" A smaller robot that walked on 4 spider like legs came from the darkness. "Now missy sissy and puppy whuppy are one, a new name must be dawned." The cackling one started to pace, smacking his head as he muttered different things to himself. He suddenly stopped raising a single finger and spinning to face them. "You are like a Chimera now, so why not be names Chimera?" He giggled to himself clapping his hands together furiously. "Chimera is a good name, no other one has the same! Such fun this new toy, it's a good girl-boy!"

Brit looked at the borg the same as Trunder, anger inside filling every fiber of their being.

The cackling one rushed over to them, flipping something on their neck.

"Daddy forgot to turn on your voice!" He laughed.

"You twisted monster" She said to him, startling herself with the new voice. The new voice a mix of a small woman's voice, a growling raspy voice, and a primitive old computer all at once.

"Oh perfect perfect, so beautiful and strong!" The cackling on danced to himself, clapping his hands once more. "Chimera is perfect!"

She had not realized it, but Trunder had stopped their body against the wall of one of the shacks behind them, snapping straight through it.

She could feel a bit of blood trickling down the leg now, a presser of what she could only believe to be pain now filling the leg as well.

"What have you done to us?" their new voice echoed through the cavern. She began scanning her memory for the files she had come to know as her own, finding none in the memory.

The cackling one grabbed at his own head. "Your mind so full of useless things, control programs, battle programs, identity files, blahhh." He did a motion of pointing one of his fingers at his mouth. "No fun, no fun. We took those and threw them away. Now it's just yours thoughts and memories left to stay." The cackling one turned away from them, beginning to skip back into the darkness. "Oh my names Tinker, but you can call me daddy now." He said as he skipped away, the metal of his feet sparking on the ground beneath him as he did.

As he slipped into the dark, once more they were alone. She and Trunder sat there for a while looking around and talking in their mind trying to understand everything that had just happened.

*   *   *

The scans showed no movement in the cursed Orotho at last. Sorton sat, tapping his new fingers against the console, thinking of what to do next. No doubt in his mind that both the Birthed and Rebirthed had taken massive casualties to these cyborgs.

"How could we lose so many?" he asked himself, sitting back in the old metal chair. "Who is the greater threat?" He asked as well.

His eyes drifted to the progress bar of the Fenrir weapon, still flashing at a 10% after 2 weeks. He slammed his hand against the console, causing its lights to flicker as a small crack formed where the hand was.

"We need something to speed this progress up!" He thought to himself, spinning his chair back to the console he had been using to research the systems. "There must be something in here that we could use until that one is finished."

He typed vigorously as he searched, scouting through the weapons and vehicles to find something. Each one he found, though useful, did not help in the current situation. He made note to go back to these after he found his answer. He turned back to the directory systems, beginning to look into the transport and building sections of the files.

He paused on something that he had to look at twice to understand what he was seeing.

"A warp device?" he asked, reading through the cryptic notes full of old human jargon he could barely understand half of. "This may be useful!" he exclaimed as he read, taking notes on each portion about the device. A section for blueprints came through after information for the device. "Classified" covered the entire section. Sorton slammed his hand against his own leg, putting cracks in his own armor.

"Classified?!" he shouted, scrolling through more of the information to find why there was no blueprint. "Only one was ever made?! Hidden on one of the humans water vessels?!" he shouted, flying to his feet. "I must have this!"

He sent a request for a few of the bots to come to the command room, waiting no more than a few moments before they appeared through the door, bowing as they entered.

"I want you and the bots in your squads to search for an old human vessel, one named Salvation!" He shouted at them.

The bots looked at one another before turning back to him and nodding a "yes sir" spoken in unison before the left the room at full speed.

"This will be mine! We will just warp soldiers and weapons into every base and destroy them from within!" He thought to himself, a small chuckle escaping him.

*   *   *

Johnny walked through the streets of Jaxfell, word of the missing bots from the human wars reaching him after many months, the bot who had told him now permanently stationed at the water front defense tower.

He had found many things during his exploration, each one more confusing than the last.

The last place they had all been seen was an old biological building, used to clone and mix plant species. It had been abandoned for a long time as new ones had been built, left to rot with age. Bullet holes and burns from lazer weapons riddled the walls and floor. Yet it was devoid of any remains. A few guard bots accompanied him to this place, each of them inspecting the areas with him.

"What happened to them?" he asked himself as he stepped from the building back into the streets. The guards who came with him did not join him outside, instead they continued inspecting the building for clues.

Johnny looked down the street at the multiple abandoned buildings of what used to be the center of Jaxfell. Remembering building these buildings with the old bots by hand. He shook of his personal feelings about it as he needed to get back to his command room for the war.

"Johnny?" a voice echoed out of one of the abandoned buildings, drawing his attention almost immediately to it.

"Yes?" he replied his hand reaching for a weapon the he did not carry. "Who calls my name?"

A small bit of laughter echoed out of the building. "You do not recognize an old friend?" the unseen bot chuckled.

"Not by voice no, show your face so I may remember!" he shouted, the guard bots now coming out of the building, weapons drawn.

One of the old bots stumbled out of the building, a bit of miss matched parts keeping him together. A closer look showed much of the bot had become cracked and rusted.

"Chaz?" Johnny exclaimed, motioning for the guards to lower their weapons. "Why are you here? Where are the others?"

Chaz chuckled, the body motion causing a bit of old oil from his systems, something that bots had not used in more than 50 years.

"Gone in a flash of lights and gunfire is where they are Johnny!" Chaz yelled, his legs struggling to keep the old bot up. "The bodies leaving no trace, and the cackling echoing through the night."

Johnny paused, nodding at what Chaz said. Motioning for the guards to gather Chaz.

"We will speak more on this, but first let's get you fixed up." Johnny tried his best to sound sorry for Chaz. The guards moving in and helping the old bot walk with them.

Johnny stood there for a moment, once more reminiscing on the past of Jaxfell before joining the guards. They walked for a while as they headed to the inner wall of the city, passing by a few different shops just outside of the gate, the bots inside whispering about Chaz and Johnny under their breath. He paid this no mind, as he knew that this was normal as he rarely left the command building these days.

They strolled through the inner gate, being greeted by lush grass fields. The beauty of this place was legendary in Jaxfell, as it was the only garden in the city. All the researched and saved plants rested in this place. A few black spires jolted through the plants into the sky.

"When did this occur with the lights and gunfire?" Johnny asked Chaz, who seemed to be lost by the beauty of the gardens.

"Last time I was here this was just grass and a few trees." Chaz whispered, a tone of awh in his voice.

Johnny thought of it, as the gardens had been here for more than 60 years at this points. "Has it really been that long?" he thought to himself as they strolled towards the approaching command building.

"The loss of the bots was shortly after the initial explosions of the city, no more than 4 or 5 days. It is hard to keep track of time with an endless day from our dome.." Chaz spat out, his body beginning to leak a bit more oil and coolant as more seals broke.

Johnny nodded to the guards as he stopped walking, the guards understanding his motion as they moved Chaz to the droid repair room.

"That would make it the same day that I had requested them to meet with me." Johnny thought, his hand going to his chin as he became lost in thought. "Who would have attacked them in Jaxfell? How would they know where to find them?"

*   *   *

Chimera became used to their name after a few days, learning to walk and work together. The cyborgs around them, aside from Tinker, all seemed rather friendly actually.

"We thought you were brutes and monsters" They said, taking a small bite from the meat of an unknown animal.

A few of the cyborgs chuckled, take a few swigs of unknown drinks.

"Nah we ain't no monstas' or brutes, just a bunch of people been stuck in this crummy sitiation for a long time!" Jerrith chuckled out, taking a large swig from his drink.

"We learned this by living here" Chimera nodded, taking another quick bite of the blue meat.

"We wonder though, what of Tinker? He seems to be mad!"

The chuckles turned to laughter, a few of them falling from what they had been sitting on to the ground, sparks flying as their metal parts struck the rock.

"He mad alright, been that way long time. We don' know what made him coo-coo but he helps us and leads us since Misfit be gone." Jerrith replied, patting Chimera's back. "Don't you pay him no no mind."

Chimera nodded and continued eating, feeling at home with these borgs. They did not care for how the cyborgs lived this long, all they cared about was the food and friendship they had with the borgs.

*   *   *

Jorge snuck around, jolting between covers. A few of the others with him doing the same. They had been looking for the human water vessel for more than 2 weeks, exploring every bit of what used to be the location it was last known to be found at.

Earlier that morning after a light fire tornado they had found its location. The troubling thing that they had found was there was already movement there. Some faint lights shined out of one of the many entrances that had rotted through it.

He moved quickly to get a better vantage point on the unknown presence, weapon at the ready. A quick scope in with his vision enhancer showed the movement was robotic in nature, though no discernable xerophia glow came from within. A few of his squad had already ventured to the ship, peeking through a few of the portholes.

They motioned for the others to come forward, signaling the all clear.

This confused Jorge, as he could plainly see movement inside the ship. He crept up as slowly as he could, trying to not make any extra sound than he needed to. He after a few moments reached one of the rotten holes, rust flakes covering the entire outskirts of the hole.

Inside was a few hanging robot systems, very primitive in nature as well as non-xerophia equipped. They climb through a few of the holes, finding a thick layer of dust caking most of the areas away from the windows and holes. The light he had been seeing, he found, was a mirror reflecting the light from the window, an odd substance altering the coloring like rainbows.

The squad moved through the ship, scanning items that seemed interesting with the odd devices that Sorton had given them, referring to them as "analytic scanners". The items once scanned displayed on a small screen on the back of the plasma pistol shaped device, breaking down the elements and seemingly the insides of each with their intended purpose.

Jorge found what looked like an old version of the databoards that the Birthed and Rebirthed seemed to use. He did not scan the item, instead simply turned it on, jumping slightly when the screen dimly clicked on.

"It still works?" he asked himself as he whipped as much of the dust off as he could. Once the screen was visible, the light was much brighter. He scanned through the information, finding it was a log of some old human experiments.

"Day 31, the experiments with dimensional changes seems to be going well. We have been able to warp people from one place to another with only milliseconds stuck in an alternate dimension. Unlike the hours from before…I still have nightmares of that moose in the white room… chewing its walnuts." The last log read, the concept confusing to Jorge. He slid the old pad into an odd metal case next to where he found it, grabbing the surprisingly un-rusted handle and caring it with him as he continued to explore the ship.

One of the others found some blueprint concepts for some weapons and exo-suites, while another found what they could only assume was some form of new explosive.

Jorge entered an old room, rather large in size. A few remains of human skeletons lay preserved in the air tight room. An odd machine seemed to encompass the entire ceiling and one of the walls. Jorge took a scan of the entire system, the device unsure of what the room was made for.

He wondered over to the command console, hoping to find a way to turn it on. Some old archaic symbols covered the hard button console, only a few of the symbols familiar to him.

He pressed a few of them, the device coming to life behind him. Jorge, unsure of what it was doing attempted to flee the room, running straight back to the door as the countdown timer that had started reached 2. He made it part of the way when a bright light surrounded him and he could feel the world beginning to separate around him.

*   *   *

Johnny watched as a strange blue sphere opened in the gardens outside, a few of the guard bots running to meet it. A loud pop emitted from the area as the sphere cleared and a bot with glowing red eyes stood in the burned area, bits of the dirt turned to glass beneath it. The bot looked around confused for a moment before the guard laid fire directly into it, sending it to the ground in a burst of metal and sparks.

Johnny laughed furiously, rushing as fast as he could down to the gardens from the command building. He passed by his old friend who raised a hand to speak to him but ignored it as he ran.

As he reached the destroyed bot, the guards had already surrounded it. The red eyed bot lay motionless as the arms and legs had already been detached from its torso. The ground cracked under each step, reflecting the sound from long ago of feet walking through the snow.

Johnny knelt next to the bot whose eyes never left his.

"A warp device huh? Sorton has found the thing we have been searching for!" Johnny laughed to himself "Now we will just have to get the information from you!" Johnny nodded to the guards who began dragging the bot back with them to the command centers interrogation room.

"What this?" he asked himself as an odd looking weapon dropped from the bot. He snatched it up, looking it over. A small screen on the back flashed the message "Unauthorized user".

Johnny ignored the message and brought it along with them to the interrogation room.

*   *   *

Chimera walked with the other borgs in the underground caverns, their feet making silent patters compared to the heavy metal and boot stomps from the others. A newly mounted weapon on their back bounced up and down with each step, the end of the lazer barrel bobbing just in the corner of their eye.

"1 day mo' and we be there" one of the borgs, seemingly a small child with a much older voice echoed out.

Chimera nodded as they continued walking, the robotic side of their mind continually running checks on the weapons and systems to ensure they are prepared for their first battle.

They had been told no more than 1 hour before leaving for the mission. It was no concern for them as they felt the need to get out into the world they loved so much. The mission they had been sent on was to go and scavenge one of the smaller robotic towns for parts for Tinker to repair the borgs or make more "toys" with.

Chimera had no concerns with doing either, as they had found with living among cyborgs a lot of what they have known about the cyborgs and humans were not entirely true. The only true concern they have had was with Tinker and his madness.

Many a time they had asked other borgs about Tinker's story, though none of them really spoke about it. Mostly giving them the response to ignore or forget it.

The walk here was not helping their inquisitive mind much, as they sought more and more to learn about their new comrades.

"We are just wishing to know more about those we fight with and for" they said to their new best friend Jerrith.

Jerrith nodded at them in the darkness of the cavern, they were only able to see it from the light emitting lightly from his eyes.

"He was once a science monkey, building up dem there body parts we be using. He even made up some dem bots that attacked and killed dem humans. Once that happened something in him snapped, giving up his own humanity to join us borgs." Jerrith paused, looking around to make sure the others were out of ear shot. "Only thing separate'n him from dem bots is his brain. Only thing left from his human self. We tend to think that be why he so crazy."

Chimera nodded as they walked, some of the pieces of the puzzle beginning to fit together. Thought they knew something was still in the past that made Tinker like he is.

"That dose help Jerrith, now what about you?" Chimera chimed up after a few moments of silence.

Jerrith stopped dead in his tracks, Chimera could barely make out the look of deep thought and confusion filling his face.

"I was something, can't fully remember doh. I remember animals and needles, fur on my clothes all the time. Make them feel good and not hurt." Jerrith started hitting his head with his closed fist. "Can't remember self, need to remember!"

Jerrith punched his head several times before a few sparks flew off and he calmed almost instantly.

"Im better now." He said and continued walked. Chimera watched this with confusion, ideas forming of memory loss and dying tissue coming to mind.

"So they become so old they cannot remember their own lives?" They thought, looking at the ground as they tried to comprehend what was going to happen to them. Shrugging it off, the continued onward to their mission.

*　　　　　　*　　　　　　*

Sorton looked over the scanned files from the returning bots. Most of the items of little to no use to them. A few different bio-weapons had promise for fighting the borgs but little use when coming to the Birthed. He stumbled on one file that perplexed him though.

"Is this it?" he asked himself as he read through the schematics of a room sized device. The scanning device had broken down the system fairly well, labeling each part based on its purpose to the device. A single item that hung from the center of the ceiling read "Wormhole Ripper".

Sorton paused upon reading this, an overwhelming bit of happiness replacing his long held anger. He read through the blue prints one more time, seeing what would be needed to get these systems working.

He had summoned a few bots in the process of memorizing the systems of the warp machine.

"I want you" Sorton pointed to the bots as they entered the room. "To build this for us."

The bots scurried over to the console, reading through the blue prints and devices.

"Manufacture the parts in our machines, halt bot production until this device is done!" Sorton excitedly shouted, shooing the bots off as the finished reading. No sooner than the click of the automatic doors closing did Sorton begin to jump and spin with excitement. "This war is ours!"

* * *

Jorge struggled against his own mind, trying to block out the memory reading devices the Birthed droids used on him. The programs attacked at his defenses, cracking through in places before his systems could clamp it with another defensive wall.

"You cannot resist long" the droid whispered to him as a large wave of files and coding began to flood his mind.

A large system breach error read across his eyes as the millions of empty files pored passed his defenses, bits of the coding for his memory escaping as the attacking code ripped into his mind.

He could feel the memories start to all fade away, but not just memories as bits of his programming for control and motor functions began to poor away. The countless empty files replaced every file in his system.

He held onto consciousness as long as he could, until the last bit of his personality file left his system.

*   *   *

Johnny watched as the droid extracted the bots systems and memories from the no doubt empty shell. The bots head fell, the lights of his eyes turning grey as the last system file left.

The thought of the same according to him fell into the back of his mind, causing a slight shiver of fear on the normally regal figure.

"It is done." The droid echoed out, quickly turning and leaving the torture room.

"It's not wright!" Chaz yelled from behind Johnny, causing him to turn furiously weapon drawn at eye level. Chaz raised his hands to show Johnny he was a friend.

"What's not wright Chaz?" Johnny asked, putting his weapon back into his side holster.

"Draining everything that made that bot himself! Bots killing bots! Everything about this Jax forsaken war!" Chaz shouted, stumbling forward on his newly fashioned legs. "We fought together against the humans, so there would be peace! Now we bring war back to this already crippled planet!"

Johnny raised his hand quickly to face level. "Enough!" he shouted at his old friend, his metallic voice echoing for a few seconds in the room and down the halls. "We did not start this war Chaz! Nor did we want to resort to torture of other bots! We have been left with no choice Chaz!" Johnny turned back to the window to the torture room, slamming his hand against the plasticized-glass.

"He had information we needed to take down the Rebirthed and Borgs once and for all!" Johnny slumped to the ground.

Chaz must have walked up to Johnny at some point, as his hand rested against Johnny's head.

"We must stop this war Johnny!" Chaz whispered, true sorrow filling his voice. "Or else it will continue endlessly as we build bots and they build bots just to be destroyed! It would continue until there was nothing left but dirt and fire!"

Johnny shrugged off the friendly hand. "That is why we must do what we are doing now!" Johnny shouted, standing back to his feet. "We will have the warp back, go straight into their base and destroy them one by one!"

Chaz looked down and shook his head with disappointment. Johnny could not take the look about his old friend, stepping out of the room with haste.

The droid who had assisted with the torture quickly approached, bouncing with excitement. "We found the blue prints and so much more to assist sir!" IT chimed out, slamming a databoard into his hands.

Johnny, attempting to ignore what had just happened with Chaz began to read the information. A giggle passed by his speaker.

"Perfect! Blue prints of the warp device as well as of their base! This war will end in a matter of days!" Johnny laughed, walking off in the direction of his quarters.

Chapter 11 – A Stalemate

Chimera sat in the darkness of the cave entrance, watching as the blue bots patrolled their outpost. None of them had been alerted to their presence. Something was amiss, that much they were sure. There were no spider tanks at the entrances, nor did it seem the gate was closed.

They slinked back into the cavern, the other borgs awaiting the scouting information turned at stared as they returned.

"The gate seems open, minimal defenses. Something isn't right." They chimed out, their whispered voices echoing gently into the caverns.

The borgs all looked at one another, the ones with still human mouths smiled.

"Then it's ours for the taking!" One from the back with the entire upper portion of his head being mechanical with the rest still being very human.

Before Chimera could protest, the borgs flew out from their cover guns firing rapidly. Chimera, against their better judgement, followed them. Their gun fired for the first time at a few of the fleeing guard bots, the jolt causing a slight tear in their shoulder. The weapons aim was true though, as the bots that had been fleeing fell into a bubbling mass of metal and coolant.

The borgs rushed for the gates, hoping its large metal blast doors had remained open as the last patrolling bot fell. They had no more than passed the threshold of the gate when a strange field surrounded the borgs, Chimera trapped on the other side from them. A strange looking device popped out from all of the walls and ceiling, large barrels pointed directly at the borgs.

Jerrith turned to look at them, a smile on his face as the barrels took alight with different shades of red, orange, blue, and purple. They looked away just as one of the plasma bursts slammed into the back of Jerrith's head, melting it away almost instantly.

Chimera fled, running back into the safety of the caverns. They never looked back even once to view the carnage that ensued behind them.

*   *   *

Fluffinator laid on an improvised couch, a few old springs that lasted the test of time burst from different locations.

He watched as Tinker giggled to himself, making a few changes to a few of the borgs. He was singing some form of the same old songs he had always sang during repairs, many of which could cause headaches to even robots.

A slight padding noise came from one of the exit caverns, the sound of paws slapping the rock. He perked his head up instantly, the newly installed plasma cannon on his back beaming to life.

A greenish furred cyborg came running into the cavern, large bullets wounds littering the sides of the legs. The borg did not seem to notice.

"They are all gone!" Chimera cried, the multiple voices seeming to mesh into one echoing screech.

Tinker laughed fairly loudly and turned to face Chimera, electric wrench still in hand.

"Chimera lived! Broken toys broke! Everything is fine, new toys will fix the problems!" Tinker laughed once more, patting Chimera on the head and turning back to his work.

Fluffinator did not have a lot of time to care about the goings on of the other borgs, as a nap felt like it needed to be done. He closed his eyes, the whine of the plasma launcher turning off helping lul him to sleep.

*   *   *

Johnny laughed as he watched the security footage one more time, slapping his own leg as the borg turned to look at the one that was separated from the other.

"The defenses work perfectly!" He shouted, one of the droids that stayed in the back of the room turned and face him. He looked at the droid, pointing a single finger from his hand at him as he fought another laugh. "Set these up both inside and out of every single city and outpost! Put them in the ground and walls!"

The droid nodded and rushed off to his console, hammering away at the keys as he fulfilled the order.

"What a week!" Johnny laughed, his electronic drug in his hand, running it gently against him as his systems began to overcharge. "First, we get a good warp blueprint, then the layout of the enemy's fort, now we found a defense even the borgs cannot surpass?!"

He looked over at the footage from the warp room they had been developing, seeing the bots work tirelessly on finishing it. He pressed a button on the feed, the intercom activating in the room.

"Progress on the warp?" He asked, pulling the drug away in time to prevent system shutdown.

One of the bots stopped his work and turned to the intercom wall.

"Another day and we will be complete sir!" It replied, turning back to its work as Johnny switched the intercom back off.

He replaced the drug onto his body, the droid around him sneaking looks here and there as he used.

"All a matter of time now!" He laughed as his body slumped down into his chair, his systems shutting down. The last thing he saw before his system rebooted was the look of Chaz in the doorway, shaking his head.

*   *   *

Sorton made a few welds on their new and improved warp device. Theirs broke away from the original blueprint, and had become mobile. A few adjustments had been made to also leave the portal running until switched off at its base which would drop the warp beam into the ground, allowing for quick getaways and the inability to be chased.

"It's finished!" he laughed as he dropped the welding device. A few of the bots who had been helping joined him in aww of the warp tower. "We must test it!"

One of the bots raised his hand to volunteer for the privilege to be the first to go. Sorton nodded to him, going to the tower base and typing in the new location for the warp to go. No sooner had he pressed the last number when the device came to life, an arch of electricity flying out from the warp drive forming an electric circle in the center.

The bot grabbed one of the shoti weapons from the other bots and jumped straight through. They watched as every molecule of the bot separated in a matter of a few milliseconds before nothing was there. Sorton turned to the armory, searching for a portable communication device finding only an old human long range radio pack. He rushed back and threw it through the warp.

No more than a few moments had passed before a signal blared in on one of the old receivers.

"I have arrived sir, it seems like an old city of sorts. According to my information I am more than 2 days walk back!" The bot yelled through the com.

Sorton nodded, an over whelming excitement coming over him as his device worked. He flicked on old switch, the mic lighting up. "Return home if you can, we will send a scouting party to meet you!" He replied to the bot, flipping the switch back off. "Halin, grab 3 other bots and go grab him. We will need him for the fights to come!"

Halin, one of the bots designed for close range combat nodded and rushed off. The others joining him. Sorton turned to look back at his warp device, laughing to himself as he walked back to his command station.

The screen reading Fenrir now read 68% across the screen, one of the droids they had reprogrammed from a fallen outpost staring indefinitely at it.

"Soon there will be no stopping us from finishing this fight!" He laughed to himself once more, his voice echoing against the walls of instruments and panels.

*   *   *

Servo reviewed over and over his new creation, his new spider like appendages helping the task be finished quicker. Some of robotic parts lay directly to his left as a slab of animal lay on his operating table. The animal seemed to be a reptile of some sort, mutated beyond what humans would have recognized as a living creature.

He did not wait nor hesitate when first given the task to make more borg animals, as Servo had been doing just that for a long time.

When he became a cyborg himself, his robotic head and mind merged with a radiated arachnid, he believed he found all the mistake he had made in his past experiments. His new one, named Crocokin, would be different because of this new knowledge.

He finished fashioning the borgs extra limbs and enhancements before switching it on.

Crocokin jolted up, as the understanding that Servo had put into him kicked in. His creation could now understand speech and orders from the borgs, as well as knowledge of what had been happening in the world that it had lived so carelessly in.

Tinker popped into the room behind him cackling and clapping as Crocokin turned to face him.

"Spinneto brought a friend! So much promise! We will have so much fun!" Tinker laughed.

Servo, now referred to as Spinneto, turned to face Tinker and joined in on the laughter. They laughed for a few seconds before Crocokin jumped down from the table, body jolting as it tried to calibrate its new body parts and functions.

"What can it do? Oh please please please tell me!" Tinker jumped and danced as he pleaded for the answers. Crocokin taking a few steps back to avoid the sparks of the feet.

"Crocokin has newly implemented lazer lined teeth, with a locking hinge attached to its jaw. The eyes have the ability to switch between night, true, sound, and heat vision, and its scaly hide has been reinforced with metal plating. The limbs have been changed by replacing the bones and joints in them with those from these old bot parts." Spinneto tapped the back of Crocokin's neck and a small hatch opened. "With attachment slot for weapons if needed."

Tinker laughed as he ran over to Crocokin, inspecting every element as much as he could.

"The new toy will last with the pew pew guns, but what about the lazers and plasma?" Tinker giggled, petting at Crocokin, who seemed to not being enjoying it.

Spinneto nodded and pointed to the spines on Crocokin's back. "The spines will most definitely be of use at that point, as in each is installed a micro shield generator. Enough to take a few lazer shots or plasma salvos with no concern!"

Tinker clapped as he hopped from one foot to the other, a quiet dink with each step. "Goody goody! Is the toy ready to play?" He asked looking at Spinneto, his head crooked to the side slightly.

Spinneto nodded as he pet at Crocokin. "He is most definitely ready!" He replied, both him and Tinker cackling a bit. Their voices echoed through the caverns around them, creating a chorus of hundreds of laughs.

*   *   *

Sorton looked over his amassed army of thousands of bots and vehicles, each face staring up at him with anticipation. He raised his hands into the air as countless voice cheered at him, weapons raised in the air before him. A few let off a few shini and blaster shots into the ceiling above, dust drifting from the newly opened holes.

"Today, we push the enemy where it counts! We moved today to end the lies and oppression of Johnny and his ilk." Sorton shouted to the masses, more cheers roaring through the base. "We move now, to cripple them where they stand. To take away from them their strength of will and controlled leadership!"

The crowds cheered once more, a few shots rang out into the ceiling once more. The bots closest to them seemed to move away from the now cracking ceiling.

"We will use this technology!" Sorton pointed to the hundreds of manufactured warp towers. "We will enter their sanctum! We will destroy them in their own homes! We will end this war and bring truth to these wastes! No more will they control their people with lies and deceit! No more will they ravage the land they claim to protect! We will go today to our victory!"

Sorton slammed his hand against the railing of his platform, the other raised in a fist above him. The others raise a single fist in the air and cheered even louder.

"We march through the warps, and unto the final battle of these lands!" Sorton finished, slamming his fist onto the railing with the other. The warp towers fired to life as their operators finished putting in the coordinates. "To Jaxfell!"

The crowd began to march towards the warps, weapons drawn to the ready.

*   *   *

Chaz wondered the grounds just outside of Jaxfell, pouring some long needed water on the crumpling grass field that had begun to grow. A series of loud pops began to echo behind him, each one accompanied with glowing lights.

He dropped his canister of water, the grass beneath seemingly reaching out to the spilled fluid for dear life. Without hesitation he hurried back to the gate as fast as he could move, hoping that what he heard was not what he believed.

He peeked his head through the gatehouse, more pops echoing throughout. More than 300 sets of red glowing eyes moved just passed the gatehouse, weapons looking around for any form of movements.

Before he could react, gunfire began to echo through Jaxfell. Several blaster and shini bots rushed into the gatehouse, weapons already firing. Chaz ducked his head back around the corner into the security room. He watched as the bots rushing from outside fired into Jaxfell, several of them getting only a single bullet out before engulfed themselves by the mix of different armaments.

Chaz looked around in the security room, hoping to find some form of weapon to defend himself with. Nothing inside the room resembled a weapon he could recognize. Instead he found the gate controls, a button labeled alarm was planted center of the console. Without hesitation his hand slammed against the button. As the loud beepings of the alarm began to go off, a large leg slammed into the gatehouse, a large plasma salvo slamming out of an unseen cannon above. The leg was met with multiple salvos itself, burning and melting the metal beneath the white hot plasma.

Chaz ducked beneath the console, slamming his back against the wall. He began to mutter different nonsense beneath his breath as fear took over his mind.

"Jax help us!" he whispered, the wall behind him erupted with plasma, melting straight through it with ease. Chaz stood and turned to face his attackers, more than 30 faced him, weapons aimed to fire.

He did not yell, nor did he plea for his life. Instead he charged straight at them, hand clenched into a fist. His body jolted with each shot that fired through his body, his legs flying out from under him as a plasma salvo burned them from his torso. His systems permanently shut off before his head his the metal below.

*   *   *

Johnny looked over the balcony, his customer shini already firing at the charging Rebirthed that managed to breach the inner wall. He counted 30 as they dropped from his fire, his weapon clicking as the clip went dry.

He leaned back into the building, dropping with clip from the weapon with a loud clank as it struck the ground, quickly replacing it with another. The guard bots in the hall with him fired out the windows as the approaching bots. Johnny turned back to balcony, taking down the last of the bots inside the grounds of the inner wall. Shells flew through the air just passed his head with each shot, the bullets meeting their targets and sending them to the scrapyard.

A loud stomp echoed from somewhere in the cityscape, followed quickly by another.

"Spider tank?" He asked himself as he scanned the horizon looking for the source of the sounds. Peeking just outside an old spare parts store was 2 large cannons. Before he could fully realize what it was he was seeing, 2 loud shots fired out. Down the hallway, a large explosion echoed out, sending a mix of bot parts and rubble flying against him, knocking him to the ground.

He stood back up as fast as he could, his sensors showing minimal damage to his body. He fired back out into the new crowd of bots flowing into the inner walls, riding on what seemed like small treaded carriers. A few of them, once shot, exploded into small explosions equivalent to a c4 packet.

A loud slam echoed in the city once more, the 2 barrels caching aflame as the plasma grazed across them. They attempted to fire, but the barrel had melted enough to cause a back fire sending the tank into a system failure. Smoke bellowed out from behind the building that it hid.

The bots in the inner walls had begun to attempt a breach into the command building, loud explosions trying to blow the blast doors from their sockets.

"Those won't hold long." Johnny thought to himself as he rushed passed them, dropping his last clip from the weapon. He rushed to the research room, a few bots working alongside the droids on the warp device.

"Is the warp device finished?!" He shouted at them as they welded away at it.

"It can warp, but will not be able to hold it for long. We need to reinforce the systems to support it!" A droid shouted, welding a small garter into place against the frame of the warp platform.

"It will have to do as it now! We will not last much longer here!" He shouted, shoving the droid aside.

A guard burst into the room, large bullet wounds covering his torso with one of his arms missing.

"Sir, they have taken down the last of our defenses in the main city. They only thing separating them from us is the blast door and sentry turrets!" The bot shouted, fighting to keep himself functioning.

Johnny nodded as he continued typing in the coordinates to one of the other cities. "We will just need more defenses then!"

No more than a few seconds after his last word a warp portal opened in the center of the room, the device beginning to shake from the strain of the portal. Without a second thought, he ran up the stairs and flung himself through the portal.

He watched as the world around him dissolved and his systems began to go haywire, errors of every kind flashing through his eyes.

Flashes and glimpses of odd things lasted a split millisecond in his vision that he could not explain.

Before he knew it, a loud pop filled his head and he was standing in the command room of one of the neighboring cities.

"Is this Cogsmin?" he spat out as he tried to get his systems back in check. The guards who had their weapons pointed at him lower them and nodded.

"Yes Johnny this is Cogsmin." A familiar voice echoed behind him.

Johnny turned to face the voice, knowing full well he would not be happy with what he seen. "We are under attack at Jaxfell." He said as Cogwill entered his vison. "We need the soldiers stationed here to join the defense!"

Cogwill laughed and nodded, his archaic modifications of cogs and gears moving and adjusting to move him forward. "We will help, that is of no concern. It tis just sad the great Johnny and the beautiful Jaxfell would need our assistance."

No more than a few words had been spoken when Johnny and more than 500 soldiers poured into the warwings. Their double adjusting engines roared to life as the last of the bots poured in. The warwings took off, doors closing as they rose from the launch pads. As they passed through the energy field, Johnny could feel every system begin to overcharge just as he had several hundred times before. He had to fight the urge to shut down as they flew to battle.

It took no more than 30 minutes before they reach the city of Jaxfell. He drew his weapon as the doors began to open. Large repeller lines shot from small holes just beneath the doors mid points, hammering into the concrete below.

Johnny could see a few of the other warwings begin to do the same, when large plasma salvos slammed into them, turning them into large flaming bubbling messes. A few of the gear modded bots grabbed the lines and slid down in front of him, firing their weapons as they repelled. He grabbed ahold of one himself, feeling like it was back in the days before the human wars ended. He leaped from the warwing, sliding down the metal wire, sparks flying as his hand gripped at the wire.

His feet slammed into the ground, a few cracks that had formed from the repeller lines grew a small bit beneath him. He ran up to the closest cover he could find, an earth colored building marked as a plant nursery. A few of the bots from his warwing joined him, their gears clanking as they ran to the cover.

Johnny peaked his head around the corner quickly, spotting 2 more of the double cannoned tanks. He slid back to cover, motioning for one of the launcher bots to take point. The bot nodded, sprinting out into the open. He did not need to take aim, as he slid to his knees and fired all 4 barrels of the launcher. The rockets flew from their ends, propelling the bot back as he was engulfed in smoke and shini gun fire.

Johnny peaked his head around the corner once more, watching as the rockets made their mark. One of the walking tanks was hit directly in their core, causing the systems to fail mid step. It fell to the side, firing the shot that had been no doubt loaded to take them out. The shot slammed into the ground not but 40 feet from them as the tanks collapsed onto the ground. The second one had been hit in the barrels, rendering its long range weapons useless.

2 large gatling guns dropped from its bottom, spinning to life as they did. Johnny poked back behind the corner as the weapons fired at them, tearing through the building they had been using for cover. A few of the bots with him exploded into sparks and rubble as the bullets shredded through the building and them. Their bodies fell to the

ground without much noise that could be audible over the loud firing of the gatling guns.

Johnny heard a ting off his shoulder, is left arm falling from his body a split second after. He dropped to the ground as the last of the bullets flew through the building. The buildings structure could not hold out as loud snaps and crumbling filled the brief silence. The top half of the building slid to its foundation, crushing a few of the still functioning bots in the process. Johnny rolled directly up to the remaining wall, the top half of the building sliding directly over him.

He lay there, listening to the now picking back up gunfire around him. He was trapped there, unaware who was winning or losing out of the building he was in.

"Will this be my end?" he thought to himself as he looked over at his destroy arm, its hand still clenching his shini.

The gunfire continued for a few more hours, slowly getting quieter and less frequent. Until suddenly it just stopped. He lay there, trying to peek out from the holes that had been formed in the wall to see if anything could be noticed in its small view.

A set of glowing blue eyes met his after a few seconds, causing him to jump back.

"We have one in here." A broken sounding voice echoed out. After a few moments, holes had been cut in the ceiling above him, 4 large bots becoming visible as it was lifted away. Cogwill peeked his head through the hole, new bullets wounds riddling his face and torso.

"So we survived, oh well I was so hoping we could make this place fancy for a change." Cogwill laughed, Johnny joining him as one of the bots lifted him out.

Johnny was sought to by the one of the repair droids, reattaching his arm as he looked around. He could not count the amount of scrap bodies he could see, bot friend and foe. The city was in shambles, many of the buildings barely standing as far as he could see. Empty shells and coolant littering the ground everywhere you looked.

Much of the plant life he could see had been destroyed or set ablaze. Some of the new plants they had made still burned in the distance of the inner gardens.

Johnny walked around a bit, looking at all the bots that still functioned. Many of them were simple bots that had been built and tasked only for plant work. Not many of the warrior bots or guards remained functioning from the battle.

He could not help but feel an overwhelming sadness as he looked over the remains of the once great city. He, with his head hung down, walked back to his command building. Smoke billowed out of the upper half from the artillery shots that destroyed most of the top 2 floors.

He walked passed the dead Rebirthed who had been mowed down by the sentry turrets. A few of the turrets sparked down on him, bullet holes covering most of them. A few bits of the building fell around him as he walked, bits of the dust landing onto the top of his head.

He wondered into the command room, the few droids that had survived already back to work. They seemed to be setting up more builder droids to make repairs to the city as well as rebuilding the army that had been lost. He sat at his command console, looking over the files of active bots from the army within the 2 cities.

The number had dropped to a mere 34 bots.

"We lost more than 4000 bots in this battle." He looked over feeds of the city, examining the destroyed buildings and gardens. "With our city all but lost."

He hung his head lower, planting his right hand onto his forehead. One of the droids scurried to him out of his peripheral vision. It startled him as it spoke.

"We have already begun work to modify our energy domes to prevent warp into the cities." The droid chipperly hammered, a look from Johnny showed a large portion of its torso had been melted away. "Should be form a counter attack?"

Johnny looked over at his console, selecting a few different cities and outposts. Multiple bots appeared on the screen, each of them doing a near double-take at the look of Johnny.

"I want you to send all troops and vehicles to the Rebirthed home base. We must destroy them now. Jaxfell has all but fallen." He did not wait for a response, he simply turned off the console. He leaned back in his chair, his head flinging back over its top. "They will pay for this choice they have made."

*   *   *

Sorton watched his perimeter cameras as hundreds of bots marched and road towards the base. He flicked a few switches, alarms sounding through the base. Only a handful of bots had been made since the initial wave had been sent. His numbers showed only about 60 were battle ready.

He looked over at the console showing Fenrir now at 89%.

"Damn" he thought as he turned back to his main console, entering a few different commands into the systems. The base showed it still had active defense systems, though time may have made much of them no longer useful.

His feed showed, after enabling the defenses, a few auto turrets and AA launchers pop from the ground. Within seconds the launchers began firing, the flying transports blowing up in a mix of flames and smoke as the rockets made impact.

A few of the tanks returned fire, melting away a few defenses. Some of the auto turrets began to fire into the crowd, taking down over 100 bots in just a matter of seconds. His own bots began showing in some of the outside feeds, firing off rockets at the spider tanks that quickly approached. Many of their shots missed, instead plowing into more of the crowds sending robotic parts and rubble flying.

The Birthed bots fired back of course, sending multiple of his own to the scrapyard. The fighting continued like this for a while before only a few of his own bots remained. The Birthed had made it almost into the base, their bodies lying no more than 20 feet from the main entrance.

Sorton sighed to himself as he looked back over to the Fenrir console, hoping in vane it had completed.

"Just a few more days it seems." He whispered as he walked away, back towards the production facilities.

Chapter 12 – The End of an Era

Johnny looked over the numbers on his console once more.

"Every bot was lost?!" he exclaimed, looking over at the droid next to him. "How it that possible?"

The droid shrugged, turning back to its numbers as it spoke. "It seems that over the 2 battles, all of our primary defense bots fell to a mix of gunfire and explosions. The only bots battle ready are those from Cogsmin."

Johnny nodded a bit, looking over the footage he could from the battles. "We will be ready next time!" He whispered to himself. He turned to the droid. "How goes the modifications to the domes?"

The droid nodded and happily spat back. "They are complete sir, no warp in or out."

Johnny nodded, until it struck him.

"We cannot warp out?! How are we to send them to distant battles quickly then?!" He shouted, slamming his fist against his chair.

The droid did not seem to mind as he turned back to his console. "The other droids have devised a new way to use the warp in the field. No worries there sir."

Johnny nodded as he looked over his console once more. "What of this information we got from the captured Rebirthed?" He asked looking over at the droid for a split second before looking back at his console.

"The Fenrir upload is nearly complete. We have managed to access the information that is streaming from the satellite back to that old base. Once they have control, we also have control." The droids replied, clicking at a few different buttons.

An image popped onto Johnny's console of the satellite and its blueprints.

"To think we would not have known of this and Sorton would have used it against us!" He thought to himself, scoffing at the thought of the Rebirthed having such control over the war.

*   *   *

Sorton looked at the 100% marker for the Fenrir project with disgust. Once more putting in the coordinates of Jaxfell for the firing location. Once more it asked for the different firing codes.

"What use are you to me?!" He shouted at the screen, slamming his fist through the console.

One of the builder bots he had made came hammering into the room, loud clanking from its heavy feet echoing through the different rooms.

"The defenses have been updated sir. New turrets and a shield generator just as you had asked." It said, saluting with its utility hand that still had the blow torch out.

Sorton nodded and looked over at the bot. "Build us this now!" He slammed a databoard against the bot, the blueprints for the Fenrir covering its screen.

The bot saluted and scurried back off to the others. Sorton looked back at his partially broken screen, trying once more to put in different codes in hopes they would work. The machine did not take them, popping up with an error of being unauthorized.

"Damn humans!" He shouted once more.

*   *   *

Chimera walked close behind Tinker and the new borg everyone had started to call Croc. They walked through a cavern that seemed so familiar to them, but they could not understand why. Tinker had been cackling the whole walk though, Fluffinator purring beside him.

When they had asked where they headed, no one had given them a direct answer. Many of them did not know themselves, only knowing it was what Tinker had told them to do. They did not like this.

"Why does this place seem familiar to us?" They asked, none of the borgs seemed to notice. Croc seemed to be the only one acknowledging they were even in the cavern.

They continued to walk for a few more hours before suddenly stopping, a small hole had been made in the cavern above them. It had been covered from the service by what looked to be concrete from one of the robotic cities. As they moved it, the distinctive glow of the energy dome of a city flooded the cavern.

Tinker stopped giggling for the first time in a very long time, placing a finger instead to the painted on mouth. Without a word, the borgs piled out into was looked like a battle ridden waste of a city. Tinker took point in front of them all, motioning to move forward into a nearby building.

Chimera followed, looking around at the buildings they seemed to remember from their past. They could not remember how they knew the places and it began to ware on them.

The building they entered was an old repair shop, some dust covered tools showed it had been long abandoned. With each step, a small gust knocked some dust of the instruments. One of them seemed to be an old oil purifier in the corner, a reflection of light coming off of its canister.

Chimera looked at their reflection for the first time since the change with utter shock. They now saw what a monstrosity they had become. Their entire head, aside from the mouth portion, had remained that of Brit. Bits of wiring fell from the head and into the back, some going to the new enhanced legs while others disappeared into their flesh. Bits of loose and broken skin hung from their belly and chest, reveling the discolored rotting flesh.

Chimera stopped for a moment, trying desperately to remember what they had looked like once. Their mind pulled up a blank, unable to understand that they had once been 2 different beings.

Tinker turned their head away from the reflection and pet their neck.

"We made you better toy, missy sissy and puppy whuppy could not do what you do!" He whispered, turning back to a large hole they had opened when Chimera had not been watching. Once more they looked at their reflection before following Tinker down into the hole.

Once in the hole the continued walked, seemingly towards the command building. Chimera knew this because their memories began to come back to them. Brit's voice separated in their mind once more from that of Trunder.

"We are home, back in Jaxfell?" Brit's voice sounded in their heads as they walked.

"We are separate again?" Trunder's growling voice echoed out for once in a long time into their mind.

They stopped for a brief moment before the borg behind them pushed them to keep going. Her memories had begun to flood back to her. Memories of finding Trunder, and how he had saved her life on multiple occasions.

Trunder too seemed to remember as visions from his perspective began to flood their mind. Something felt wrong about their situation to them now. Something seemed to be missing from them.

Tinker waddled in front of them, the image bringing more memories of the destruction of the other bots they had seen. Anger had begun to form with them as they walked, remembering they had not asked to be put like this. Remembering their own ambitions for life.

Before a word could be said another hole opened in the cavern, this time no light greeted them, instead a dark empty room.

They looked at thinker, teeth snarling at him. He seemed to notice but not care as much, as he seemed too pre-occupied with what he was doing. They looked at what he was looking at and their heart leaped.

They now noticed they were in the command building, directly behind the area where Johnny sat in the command room. The droids in the room did not seem to notice their intrusion. Nor did Johnny. Tinker crept up behind the bot, an elctro drug wand lay lazily in his lap.

"Johnny!" They shouted, the droids stirred, turning to face the voice and fleeing within a matter of a few split seconds. The bot in the chair popped up with surprise, his eyes flickering as his systems fought to stay online.

Tinker cackled wildly before jamming the electro drug into Johnny's face, sending him to the ground. The borgs now all turned to them, weapons drawn and aimed.

"Chimera is being a bad one! Chimera gets punished now!" Tinker shouted, jamming the drug into their mouth, knocking them out almost instantly.

*   *   *

Sorton passed back and forth, waiting for the builders to finish. They had not been working long, and had told him it would be weeks before the Fenrir could be completed. He did not care, as his patients had run out long ago.

"Why must this blasted thing take so long?!" he shouted at himself as he passed, his metal feet clanking against the metal of the build room and the concrete of the halls.

Something stirred behind him, his first instinct to turn and face it. What he was is not what he expected. A cyborg stood in front of him. A wild painted on smile looking directly back at him.

"Hello!" it shouted, pulling out a rod of some kind from its back. "Goodbye!" it shouted as it slammed the rod into his face.

His systems shut down almost immediately.

*   *   *

Johnny's vision once more returned to find a cavern of some sort. Old human buildings where around them in some form, as many of them seemed to be destroyed. A single hole well above him shined down at him.

He tried to move, finding his arms and legs had been bound to something behind him. He tried to look, but his head movement would not allow such a rotation.

In front of him was a rad wolf of some kind, with the upper head of a robot. It too seemed to be restrained, though it was to a wall.

The thing he was bound to stirred behind him.

"Hello?" He whispered, trying once more in vain to see what or who it was.

"Johnny?!" A not happily familiar voice echoed back to him.

"Sorton!" He whispered with disgust. "I should have known it was you!"

He struggled to get away, though the binding kept him in place.

"What have you done to us Johnny?! Who was that bot with the painted smile?!" Sorton shouted, the rad wolf now seeming to stir.

"I did not send him Sorton!" Johnny shouted back in respite.

An eary sounding voice came from somewhere in the dark.

"No I sent him!" The voice echoed. "I sent him to gather the 2 of you for me!"

A figure stepped into the light of the hole from above and out from the shadows of the building. A nearly fully human head, with the exception of its eyes, sat atop a almost perfectly built robotic body. The limbs and torso fully plated in armor, only revealed through slits and cuts in the clothing he wore.

"And who are you?!" Both Johnny and Sorton shouted at the same time.

The figure laughed, placing his hand over his face to slick back his hair.

"My name is Graves. Son of Misfit, leader of the Survivors. Now acting leader of the Survivors since his death!" He shouted, bowing slightly.

"Why have you brought us here?!" Sorton shouted, struggling against Johnny and the bonds.

Graves laughed, sliding out from inside his clothing an old looking blaster weapon.

"I have come to destroy you both, end this war, and bring about a new age of man and cyborgs of course!" Graves chuckled, taking a few steps towards them. The smiling face of the cackling one popped out from the dark, laughing with every ounce of strength in his systems.

Johnny could not see him, be he knew Graves was behind him, as the rad wolf growled in their direction. Sorton flailed as much as he could in the binds. A loud click followed by a woosh echoed in the cavern. Sorton stopped struggling.

Johnny began to kick and struggle wildly as he saw Graves come around to him.

"Now now, don't make this difficult! We want to make the planet safe again! A place we can call home! We have lived underground for far too long!" Grave shouted, placing the blaster square between Johnny's eyes.

He heard the click, then everything stopped. The last thing he saw was a flashing dim light then his systems shut off with a glimpse of an error flashing in his eyes.

*   *   *

Chimera watched as the 2 leaders were destroyed, struggling against their own restraints. Graves looked over at them now, weapon still clenched in his hand.

"Now what do we do with you?" He asked himself allowed, placing the barrel of the gun to his chin. "Can we salvage you? Or are you just a hopeless cause?"

Tinker skipped over to them, still cackling wildly. "We can always brake them again!" He laughed.

Graves nodded, tilting his gun back and forth as he tried to make up his own mind.

"Yes we could, but then again we could just make a whole new one as we did with fluffy." Grave groaned, scratching at his head with the barrel of the gun.

Chimera looked around wildly, knowing this could very well be their end again.

"We can do better, we had a lapse in judgment!" They pleaded, bowing down to Graves.

Grave growled a little and turned away. Tinker looking back and forth between them. This went on for a few moments before graves turned around to face them once more.

"Fuck it, let's make a new one!" He laughed, pointing the weapon.

Tinker cackled wildly as Chimera shut of their vision. A click echoed in their brain end then an intense head and pain filled them for a split second. Then nothing as everything went black. The echo of the cackling following them to the nothingness.

Afterword

The end did not come to the war as Graves had hoped. Instead Johnny and Sorton had been quickly replaced by new leadership. Cogwill took over ownership of Jaxfell, while one of the last surviving researchers for Sorton was his replacement.

New statues had been built in their Honor. The new Rebirthed leader, referred to by most as Joshua, lead the Rebirthed into a few victories over the Birthed soldiers. With each victory a new town or outpost was taken, expanding their ground farther and farther from their original base.

The Survivors, though struck by the fact the war continued, never stopped their experiments and attacks. The Birthed and Rebirthed had become wise to their new enemies tactics as they had built blocking fields, similar to the energy domes, under the ground to prevent a repeat of the fall of Johnny and Sorton.

Each side had begun to decipher tactics of the other, trying new things here and there to a mix of success and failure.

Heroes arose and fell for the conflicts, over small skirmishes.

A.W. The Endless Conflict

One thing still remains untapped by both the Birthed and Rebirthed, as memories fade of the much sought after Fenrir.

With the end of the Era of Johnny arises a new Era of Cogwill.

Check for the third book and conclusion to the Automiton Wars : The Beginning trilogy

Automiton Wars : A New Era

Made in United States
Orlando, FL
22 February 2022

15024567R10186